PHILIP ALLAN

LITERATURE GUIDE

FOR GCSE

A VIEW FROM THE BRIDGE

ARTHUR MILLER

Shaun McCarthy

With thanks to Jeanette Weatherall for reviewing the manuscript of this book.

Philip Allan Updates, an imprint of Hodder Education, an Hachette UK company, Market Place, Deddington, Oxfordshire OX15 0SE

Orders
Bookpoint Ltd, 130 Milton Park, Abingdon, Oxfordshire OX14 4SB
tel: 01235 827720
fax: 01235 400454
e-mail: uk.orders@bookpoint.co.uk
Lines are open 9.00 a.m.–5.00 p.m., Monday to Saturday, with a 24-hour message answering service. You can also order through the Philip Allan Updates website: www.philipallan.co.uk

ISBN 978-1-4441-1028-9
First printed 2010

Impression number 5 4 3 2 1
Year 2015 2014 2013 2012 2011 2010

Cover photo reproduced by permission of Joseph Verhey/Fotolia

Printed in Spain

Hachette UK's policy is to use papers that are natural, renewable and recyclable products and made from wood grown in sustainable forests. The logging and manufacturing processes are expected to conform to the environmental regulations of the country of origin.

P01673

Contents

Getting the most from this book and website

How to use this guide

You may find it useful to read sections of this guide when you need them, rather than reading it from start to finish. For example, you may find it helpful to read the *Plot and structure* section in conjunction with the play or to read the *Context* section before you start reading the play. The sections relating to assessments will be especially useful in the weeks leading up to the exam.

The following features have been used throughout this guide:

Target your thinking

- **What are the play's main themes?**

A list of **introductory questions** to target your thinking is provided at the beginning of each chapter. Look back at these once you have read the chapter and check you have understood each of them before you move on.

Build critical skills

Broaden your thinking about the text by answering the questions in the **Pause for thought** boxes. They are intended to encourage you to consider your own opinions in order to develop your skills of criticism and analysis.

Pause for thought

Pay particular attention to the **Grade booster** boxes. Students with a firm grasp of these ideas are likely to be aiming for the top grades.

Grade ***booster***

Key quotations are highlighted for you, and you may wish to use these as evidence in your examination answers. Page references are to the play as printed in the Penguin edition *A View from the Bridge/All My Sons*. (ISBN 978-0-141-18350-3).

Key quotation

Eddie Carbone had never expected to have a destiny.

Be exam-ready

The **Grade focus** sections explain how you may be assessed and distinguish between higher and foundation responses.

Grade ***focus***

Get the top grades

Use the **Text focus** boxes to practise evaluating the text in detail and looking for evidence to support your understanding.

***Text* focus**

Develop evaluation skills

Review your learning

Use the **Review your learning** sections to test your knowledge after you have read each chapter. Answers to the questions are provided in the final section of the guide.

Test your knowledge

Don't forget to go online for further self-tests on the text:
www.philipallan.co.uk/literatureguidesonline

Introduction

How to approach the play

A play written for stage tells a story through performance. When you read it on the page you must try to imagine it being acted on stage: the actors moving about, the scenery around them and the lights changing. If possible, try to see a live performance or a film of the play — this will make it come alive for you.

The playwright makes the audience want to know what is going to happen next — especially just before the break between Acts 1 and 2 in a two-act play like *A View from the Bridge*. In order to follow the storyline, you need to understand exactly how events in and around the Carbone house unfold and how the characters develop throughout the play. The timeline at the beginning of the *Plot and structure* section of this guide will help you, but it is good idea to keep your own notes as you read through the play so that you have the structure of the story clear in your mind.

However, if you want to gain a high mark in the exam it is not enough just to know what happens in the play. You must understand the deeper and more complex elements the playwright, Arthur Miller, is trying to explore through Eddie Carbone's story.

A View from the Bridge is set in a time and place that is relatively remote to people in Britain today. The characters are living in the 1930s in a city across the Atlantic Ocean and in a community that has now more or less vanished. Yet Miller wanted to write a play that would have meaning for audiences in different times and places. He explores themes that are very much part of life today: the experience of the immigrant, the difference between law and natural justice, the implications of living by an idea of honour, and the nature of love. All these themes have relevance far beyond the crowded apartment houses and streets of Red Hook.

There are no references to dates in the play to tell us exactly when the story is supposed to take place. The song 'Paper Doll', sung by Rodolpho in the play, was number one in the *Billboard* chart in the USA from November 1943 to January 1944. As Christmas takes place around the middle of the play, we might think Miller set the play during the time that song was top of the charts. However, at this time the Second World War was raging, with Italy fighting against the USA, Great Britain and the other Allied nations. No merchant shipping was then operating between enemy countries and it is unlikely that Miller would not refer to the war, if the play had been set at that time. The most likely explanation is that Miller imagines the play happening just before the war, in the late 1930s. 'Paper Doll' was actually written in the 1920s, so maybe Rodolpho was ahead of popular culture in already knowing the song!

To gain a good mark you need to be able to explore and explain how Miller creates believable and complex characters. Playwrights cannot speak directly to their audience in the way that the author of a novel can. Everything has to come through the mouths of the characters. In *A View from the Bridge* Miller is exploring complex themes, yet his characters are ordinary men and women who do not have the education to express themselves using complex vocabulary. Instead, Miller conveys his themes through a combination of raw, at times violent, dialogue and well-structured plot and action. The *Characterisation* and *Style* sections of this guide will help you understand how Miller achieves this.

Corel

The Statue of Liberty: a symbol of hope for immigrants arriving in New York by boat

Using the text to develop your own ideas

You will not gain a good mark if you just copy the ideas in this guide without thinking about them yourself, although you will of course be dealing with the same material when creating good, high-scoring answers of your own. The key to using the text of the play well is to select the correct quotations to explain the points you are trying to make. You need to know the play in detail in order to see where these quotations are. When answering a question about law versus natural justice, for example, you should be able to identify immediately that some of the best quotations about this theme are to be found in the conversation in which Alfieri persuades Marco to accept bail so that he can work back at the docks until he is deported (pp. 78–79).

You will gain marks if you show understanding of how the text is designed to be used by a theatre company to create a stage production.

Understanding how Miller uses stage directions to add clarity to what he wants characters to express is important. If you have seen live or recorded versions of the play, you should note points from each production that show how Miller tells a story through dramatic performance. You might, for example, comment on how there are no scene breaks in either act; the action flows from one scene, one place and time, straight into the next.

Context

- What is the context of the play?
- How did Miller's own life influence the play?
- How did the experiences of the Italian immigrant community in New York create the background for events in the play?
- How did the play develop from Miller's original into the work you are studying?

The Italian immigrant experience in New York

New York consists of five large boroughs or districts. The best known is Manhattan, with its towering skyscrapers and famous sites like Times Square and Central Park. It is the shopping, entertainment and business heart of the city. In *A View from the Bridge* Catherine says she has hardly ever been there and Rodolpho says he dreams of seeing its bright lights. To many poor immigrants to America in the twentieth century, the cityscape of Manhattan represented a dream of wealth and sophistication.

Of course most people in New York lived outside Manhattan in one of the other four less wealthy, more residential boroughs. Like most immigrants, those arriving — legally or illegally — from poverty-stricken Sicily and southern mainland Italy settled among people originating from the same areas as themselves. New York is still famous for having many different ethnic-minority communities. There is a 'Little Italy' neighbourhood in Manhattan itself. Most Italian immigrants, however, ended up living in cheap-to-rent apartments across the other side of the wide East River from Manhattan, in Brooklyn. The title of the play refers to the idea of looking from the Brooklyn Bridge down across the docks at Red Hook.

National Archives

A workman looks down at the lights of Manhattan from a skyscraper under construction. What does this view represent for Rodolpho?

Red Hook — the world of the play

At the time when the play is set, Brooklyn housed one of the biggest Italian immigrant communities in the world. There were Italian shops, churches and restaurants. People from poor villages in Sicily and southern mainland Italy brought their customs and their ideas of community to America. Although such a tight-knit community could look after 'its own' people — as Eddie and Beatrice look after the cousins when they arrive — there were also elements within the community who exploited their own countrymen.

Pause for thought

Marco and Rodolpho are brought to the house by 'Tony', whose one line in the play is a curt instruction to the cousins, 'I'll see you on the pier tomorrow. You'll go to work.' We assume he is one of the gang who has smuggled them into America and that they will have to do as he says. He walks away without saying another word, no 'goodbye' or 'good luck'. What sort of impression does he create?

Criminal gangs extorted money from businesses by operating protection rackets, whereby a gang offered to 'protect' your premises from damage or attack, which they themselves would cause if you didn't pay them! Many of these gangs were made up of Italians preying on fellow countrymen who had started businesses. Dockworkers were exploited when corrupt deals to keep wages low were made by the dockworkers' unions with managers. Many of the local union branches were run by Italians. Immigrants were exploited by Italian gangs that smuggled them into America, which charged their countrymen large sums for the journey then got them low-paid jobs in the docks and took the money back over months or even years.

Key quotation

RODOLPHO [*to* EDDIE]: He says we start to work tomorrow. Is he honest?

EDDIE [*laughing*]: No. But as long as you owe them money, they'll get you plenty of work. (p. 27)

Even after years of living in America and finally gaining a bit more than a living wage each week, many Italian immigrants stayed within communities where they felt at home. Eddie and Beatrice are like this: we never learn how long they have been in New York, or even if they might have been born there. (They are legal American citizens.) It does not matter that we do not know because the important thing about Eddie is that he is a typical man of his community. He lives by a code of honour that comes straight from the villages of Sicily. Living in Red Hook and being an American citizen has not changed him.

Arthur Miller — playwright and radical

Arthur Miller was born in 1915 in New York. His family were Polish–Jewish immigrants. He led a more exciting and varied life than many writers. He became a hugely successful playwright, but only after such a long struggle to get his first works produced in theatres that he was on the verge of giving up.

He became a famous public figure when his plays were produced on stage to great acclaim through the late 1940s. In 1956 he married the Hollywood film star and sex symbol Marilyn Monroe. A famous headline in one American newspaper described their marriage with the words 'Egghead Marries Hourglass', referring to his supposed cleverness and her sexy figure!

Miller had strong left-wing political opinions. He gave his support to exploited workers fighting against corrupt management and politicians. This got him into trouble with the United States government in 1950 when it was conducting 'witch-hunts' against suspected communists in America. Miller made no secret of his support for many political ideas that the United States government thought dangerous. Perhaps not coincidentally, this was the same year he adapted a play by Norwegian playwright Henrik Ibsen (1828–1906) called *An Enemy of the People*.

Pause for thought

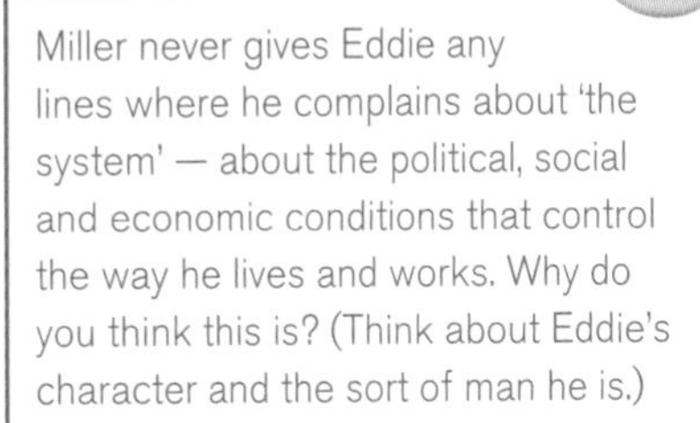
Miller never gives Eddie any lines where he complains about 'the system' — about the political, social and economic conditions that control the way he lives and works. Why do you think this is? (Think about Eddie's character and the sort of man he is.)

Grade ***focus***

A C-grade student writing about how Miller's political views influence the story might simply describe how he shows the hard life men like Eddie were forced to lead. An A*-grade student would use their background reading about the author's life and works to show how other plays Miller wrote were influenced by the same political opinions, notably his most famous play *The Crucible*.

Miller was called before the notorious House Un-American Activities Committee (HUAC). He was asked to name people he had met at left-wing political meetings in the 1930s. He refused and was fined, though the fine was later cancelled by the Supreme Court. Some 'patriotic' newspapers and members of the public voiced their suspicion of him. Many other famous writers, filmmakers and actors did not take a stand such as Miller's and named people they had associated with.

Key quotation

I mean, in the worst times, in the worst, when there wasn't a ship comin' in the harbour, I didn't stand around lookin' for relief — I hustled.

(Eddie, p. 49)

In a sense Miller had the last word against HUAC. In 1953 he wrote his best-known play *The Crucible,* about witch trials in colonial America. The 'witches' are innocent women condemned on unreliable testimonies and judged by a frightened and bigoted community. The parallels between this plot and the work of HUAC were obvious.

Despite being regarded as one of the world's greatest dramatists by the mid-1950s (*A View from the Bridge* was first staged in the United States in 1955–56), to some ordinary Americans he remained little better than a traitor. Although Miller lived all his life in the United States, he said

that even in the 1980s, when he was an old man, many Americans still distrusted him.

Miller's autobiography, *Time Bends,* was published in 1987. It is a very vivid account, not just of his life but of the American society in which he lived and wrote his plays.

Arthur Miller died in 2005. He was still writing new plays right up to the end of his life.

How Miller's own life influenced the play

In the early 1940s, before he was a successful dramatist, Arthur Miller spent two years working alongside Italian–American and other immigrants in the dockyards of New York, giving him great understanding of how they lived, before he began writing *A View from the Bridge*.

He discovered that dockworkers (or 'longshoremen') were very poorly paid. The dock management and the unions (which were supposed to protect their members) often collaborated in deals that kept wages low and working conditions poor. Few men had the security of a regular, full-time job. The number of men required each day varied according to what ships arrived and needed unloading. Men had to register for a card allowing them to work, then waited each morning by the dock gates in a crowd and were chosen, or not, by a gangmaster for work that day. Usually some men were left standing idle. If a man was considered a troublemaker by the unions or the bosses, he could find himself without work day after day.

Pause for thought

On p. 29 Eddie tells Marco that he could make 'thirty, forty a week'. Marco is delighted, yet the Carbone household live quite frugally, so $40 is not a big wage in New York. What does Marco's reaction indicate about the life he has left behind?

Miller was appalled by this exploitation. He saw that by creating this uncertainty, dock managers were making sure the men would not organise and fight for better pay and conditions. A similar theme is explored in the 1954 film *On the Waterfront* starring Marlon Brando. This graphically depicts the struggles against the corrupt system by men working in the New York docks.

Many dockworkers were illegal immigrants who could not complain to the authorities about exploitation. They had to pay back the money they owed to the gangs which had smuggled them into America. These gangs arranged jobs in the docks for the illegal immigrants, but as soon as their debts were paid off (which could take a very long time) the men were left to fend for themselves.

For many immigrants, legal or illegal, life was hard, but it was even worse back in Sicily and southern mainland Italy, so there was a steady flood of immigrants up to the Second World War (1939–45), when Italy's fascist government sided with Hitler against Britain, the USA and the other Allies. At this time all sea traffic between America and Italy stopped.

Miller became friendly with some of the men he worked with in the docks. This gave him the insights that he used to create the characters and the background to *A View from the Bridge*. Two stories he heard gave him the raw material for the play. In the first, a man confided to Miller that he had a dream in which he had a strange attraction to his female cousin. Miller suggested to the man that he might have an unconscious desire to have an incestuous relationship with her. The man was horrified at this explanation and refused to accept it.

The second story Miller heard was that of a man who betrayed to the authorities two of his own relatives who had come to New York illegally. He did this because he was furious about a growing relationship between one of the men and his niece.

The 2007 Italian film *Golden Door* graphically depicts the poverty in Italy from which immigrants fled and the journey they made across the Atlantic in over-crowded ships to the immigrant processing centre on Ellis Island in New York Bay.

TopFoto

The deck of a boat crowded with Italian migrants heading for America in 1900. Why was America such a popular destination for poor Italians?

Different versions of the play

The version of *A View from the Bridge* you are studying is very different from the play in its original form. Plays often go through extensive changes and rewrites as they are developed into a stage production.

At the time he was writing the play, Miller was interested in Greek tragedies. These ancient dramas follow very formal rules for characterisation and structure. Miller experimented with using some of these rules in modern writing for the stage. He thought the timeless quality of Eddie Carbone's tragic story might be suited to the ancient forms.

Miller's first version of the play was written in one act. Instead of the naturalistic speech of the characters, it was written in verse and was more melodramatic than realistic. This one-act version was performed in America where it received very mixed reviews.

Miller knew this stylised version of the story was not working. He brought the play to London and rewrote it in the form we know today. This more naturalistic two-act version was very well received by audiences and critics when it opened in a London theatre.

Review your learning

1. What is meant by the context of a play?
2. What made America so appealing to Italian immigrants?
3. What special problems did illegal immigrants face in America?
4. What reaction might 'ordinary Americans' with little knowledge of the immigrant communities have towards the play?

(See answers on p. 85.)

More interactive questions and answers online.

Plot and structure

- What are the main events in the play?
- How do these unfold in sequence through the play?
- How does Miller structure the play to help us understand its themes as well as follow the action?
- How do characters' wants and drives push the story forward?
- What is the timeline of events in the play?

The two-act structure

A View from the Bridge is a two-act play. In a stage production there is almost always an interval between the two acts. This is a key moment in the plot of the play — not just a chance for the audience to get up and stretch their legs.

It is the point where events that will trigger the climax of the story gather force and speed. We usually have an idea at the end of Act 1 of what might happen in Act 2 and how the story will conclude in general terms; happily or tragically. The last moments of Act 1 should contain a dramatic event that poses a question that the audience will be keen to see answered. In *A View from the Bridge* the dramatic event is Marco challenging Eddie to lift a chair by its leg, and making Eddie look weak. This leaves the audience thinking 'How will Eddie react to losing face to Marco?' This is the first time in the play that Eddie has not been in charge of things, the first time he has been challenged as a man by another man.

The first act of a two-act play is usually longer than the second because the first act has to set up the world of the play, introduce the main characters (it is very rare for a play to introduce a significant new character in the second act) and develop the story up to a crucial point. It is also better for the theatre audience to have a shorter second act; it makes a more satisfying theatrical experience.

Timeline

Pages	What happens	Timing
Act 1		
11–13	Alfieri introduces the world of the play.	Unclear — he is looking back to the whole story so it has all already taken place.
13–16	Eddie comes home. Catherine shows her new clothes. Eddie disapproves. Eddie tells Beatrice her cousins have arrived.	Early evening, day 1
16–26	Eddie, Beatrice and Catherine discuss her going to work. They tell the story of Vinny Bolzano.	The same evening
26	Narration by Alfieri.	
26–33	The cousins arrive and talk of life back in Italy. Rodolpho sings.	10 p.m. the same evening
33	Narration by Alfieri.	
34–36	Eddie and Beatrice discuss Catherine and Rodolpho going out. Eddie tells Beatrice he does not like Rodolpho. She complains about their sexless marriage.	Evening, after 'weeks [have] passed'
36–38	Louis and Mike discuss the cousins with Eddie.	The same evening
38–42	Eddie warns Catherine that Rodolpho would only marry her to gain citizenship.	The same evening
42–45	Beatrice tells Catherine to act like an adult. She introduces the idea of Catherine and Rodolpho marrying.	The same evening
45–50	Eddie visits Alfieri to find out if there is a law that can stop the marriage.	Alfieri says the visit was 'at this time', so it must be soon after recent events
51–58	Eddie, Beatrice, Catherine, Rodolpho and Marco in the house. Rodolpho talks about working on fishing boats. He and Catherine dance. Eddie becomes angry. He boxes with Rodolpho. Marco lifts the chair.	It is not clear how many days have passed since Eddie visited Alfieri
Act 2		
59	Alfieri introduces Act 2.	23 December. It is not clear how much time has passed since the end of Act 1
59–63	Catherine and Rodolpho are alone in the house. He takes her to the bedroom.	The same day

63–65	Eddie arrives. He throws Rodolpho out. Catherine sides with Rodolpho.	The same day
65–67	Eddie's second visit to Alfieri.	27 December
67	Eddie phones the Immigration Bureau.	The same day
67–73	The cousins have moved. Eddie and Beatrice argue about their marriage and about Catherine and Rodolpho marrying.	Unclear — probably the next day
73–77	Marco, Rodolpho and the Lipari brothers are arrested. Marco spits on Eddie. Everyone realises what Eddie has done and why.	Unclear — the next day?
77–79	Alfieri bails Marco and Rodolpho. Rodolpho's marriage to Catherine is arranged to take place at once.	Unclear — probably the next morning
80–83	Beatrice and Catherine try to persuade Eddie to come to the wedding. Catherine turns against Eddie. Rodolpho tries to make peace with Eddie.	Unclear — probably the same day
83–85	Marco confronts Eddie in the street. They fight. Eddie dies.	The same day
85	Alfieri talks of how he remembers Eddie.	The same 'future' time as his speech at the start of the play

Act 1 (pp. 11–33)

- Alfieri as narrator introduces himself and the world of the play. He hints that this is going to be a story with a tragic ending.
- Catherine greets Eddie as he comes home from the docks. He tells her to act in a more reserved way.
- Catherine and Beatrice persuade Eddie to let Catherine go to work.
- Eddie tells Beatrice that her cousins Marco and Rodolpho have landed. They are illegal immigrants from Italy.
- Eddie and Beatrice tell the story of Vinny Bolzano.
- The cousins arrive at the house. Eddie is unhappy at the interest Catherine shows in Rodolpho, who he instantly dislikes.

Alfieri's poetic opening speech introduces us to the world of the play. He also introduces some key themes of the story that go far beyond the Italian community of 1930s New York.

At the end of his speech Alfieri introduces Eddie, who has appeared on another part of the stage. Alfieri speaks in the past tense. This suggests that the lawyer is looking back to events that have happened. His last line mentions the open sea, the ocean that leads all the way back to Sicily

where most of the characters come from, bringing with them the ideas of honour and pride that will trigger the play's tragic ending.

Pause for thought

Although he is generally an authoritarian and demanding 'head of the house', Eddie shows, especially in the early scenes of Act 1, that he has a humorous side. He jokes that Beatrice is too kind-hearted and would turn them both out their bed to give relatives in trouble somewhere to sleep (pp. 16–17). How would you describe Eddie's style of humour?

The lights come up to show the house (actually a ground floor apartment) where most of the play will take place. Catherine, Eddie's 17-year-old niece, greets him eagerly as he comes home from the docks. She is wearing a new skirt and has done her hair in a new style. She knows she looks attractive and wants Eddie to see this. He tells her she is beautiful, but quickly says she is showing herself too much to the young men in the tough neighbourhood. She should be more cautious and reserved. We can see how she is growing up and wants to be noticed, but we can also see that Eddie may have a point, for this is a rough neighbourhood and she is perhaps unaware of the effect she has on young men. We don't yet know that Eddie is overprotective of his niece because he notices her sexual attractiveness in a way that he, as her guardian, should not.

Photostage

Alfieri (left, Allan Corduner) and Eddie (Ken Stott) in the 2009 production at the Duke of York's Theatre, London. Why does Eddie struggle to express himself to the lawyer?

Key quotation

Katie, you are walkin' wavy...The heads are turnin' like windmills.
(Eddie, p. 14)

Eddie tells Beatrice, his wife, that her two cousins have landed. They are illegal immigrants. They will stay with Eddie and Beatrice and be given work on the docks by the gangs that have smuggled them to America. They have to pay off the cost of this illegal journey. The cousins have landed earlier than expected, and Beatrice is worried that the house is not ready for guests.

Catherine tells Eddie she has been offered a job as a stenographer at a plumbing firm. She is keen to go out to work and earn money but Eddie is against the idea. He thinks she ought to finish her college course, but he also says the men who work at the plumbing company and the men on the streets she will walk along to get to work will take too much notice of her. Within a few moments, Eddie has gone back to talking about how Catherine looks and how men see her. Beatrice sides with Catherine, and Eddie finally agrees that she can take the job. Catherine is overjoyed.

Over dinner, Eddie warns the two women to be careful now they have illegal immigrants staying with them. He treats them as if he knows more about the 'real world' than they do.

Eddie and Beatrice recall the story of a local boy who informed on his own uncle to the immigration authorities. This conversation gives a hint of the complex codes of honour and justice that the Italian–American community live by, where a family will attack its son because he acts in a dishonourable way.

Beatrice is sharp with Eddie as she clears the table. This is caused partly by the sight of Catherine sitting on the ground beside Eddie like a little girl, and partly by something that will be revealed as the play progresses. Eddie and Beatrice's marriage has not been a happy and sexually fulfilled one for some time. When we think about the whole play, we see that Beatrice suspects that some of Eddie's loss of interest in her is because he is thinking of his niece in a sexual way.

Key quotation

You don't understand; you still think you can talk about this to somebody just a little bit. Now lemme say it once and for all, because you're makin' me nervous again (Eddie, p. 22)

Grade ***focus***

A C-grade student using evidence from this scene to answer a question about the relationships between Eddie, Beatrice and Catherine would end their analysis by saying that Eddie and Beatrice are uneasy with each other. An A*-grade answer to the same sort of question would however point out that the 'natural order' of the Carbone house is restored as the scene crosses into the next one with Alfieri. Eddie is resting, the women doing housework. Eddie has got his way, asserted his authority in his domestic domain. This moment neatly closes the scene down. The student writing an A*-grade answer is showing they understand how scenes are constructed for dramatic effect.

Alfieri appears again. He says that Eddie was a good, hard-working man — note the past tense again. He mentions that the cousins came as planned at ten o'clock. This keeps alive the sense of events running their inevitable course.

Marco and Rodolpho are warmly received into the Carbone house. Catherine is amazed at Rodolpho's blond hair. The cousins talk about their poverty-stricken lives in Italy. Marco has left behind a wife and three children. He wants to work to send money home. Rodolpho is unattached and much more carefree. He wants to become an American. He talks

Pause for thought

In a stage play, actions add to the meaning and drama of the story. Explain the significance of Catherine pouring sugar into Rodolpho's cup and Eddie's look (p. 33).

about his brief singing career and then he sings for everyone. Eddie is immediately disturbed by Catherine's interest in Rodolpho. He makes her change the high heels she has put on to welcome the cousins.

Act 1 (pp. 34–58)

- Weeks later, Catherine and Rodolpho are going out. Eddie tells Beatrice he does not like Rodolpho. Beatrice complains to Eddie about their sexless marriage.
- Louise and Mike discuss the cousins with Eddie.
- Eddie warns Catherine that Rodolpho would only marry her to gain citizenship.
- Beatrice tells Catherine to act like an adult. She introduces the idea of Catherine and Rodolpho marrying.
- Eddie visits Alfieri to find out if there is a law that can stop the marriage.
- Eddie, Beatrice, Catherine, Rodolpho and Marco in the house. Rodolpho talks about working on fishing boats. He and Catherine dance. Eddie boxes with Rodolpho. Marco lifts the chair.

Pause for thought

What does Alfieri mean when he says 'Now, as the weeks passed, there was a future'?

Key quotation

Eddie Carbone had never expected to have a destiny. (Alfieri, pp. 33–34)

With the picture of Eddie looking 'pained' at Catherine and Rodolpho fading into darkness, the lights come up on Alfieri in his office. He is a kind of wise onlooker. His short speech on pp. 33–34 contains simple philosophy about the kind of lives that men like Eddie lead. Again, Alfieri leaves us with a sense of foreboding.

The last line of Alfieri's speech tell us that a few weeks have passed. Eddie is waiting for Catherine and Rodolpho, who have gone to the cinema. Beatrice arrives, and Eddie tells her that he is worried about the relationship that has developed between his niece and her cousin. Beatrice cannot understand why Eddie increasingly dislikes Rodolpho. He struggles to explain his feelings. He says Rodolpho makes him feel uneasy. Rodolpho sings when he works on the ships and makes jokes. The other men call him 'Paper Doll' after the popular song he likes to sing. Eddie thinks Rodolpho is effeminate, is not a typical tough Italian–American male. He even dislikes Rodolopho's blond hair: almost all Italians have dark hair.

Beatrice tells Eddie not to worry about Rodolpho, but to tell her why he shows no sexual interest in her any more: they haven't made love for three months. Eddie will not explain.

Eddie meets Louis and Mike, two men he works with on the docks. They tell Eddie that Marco is a strong worker but that

Pause for thought

Alfieri's remark about 'destiny' tells us a lot about how he regards Eddie and the men like him who live in Red Hook. Their lives are driven by hard work. In this world, Eddie is a good man, he has looked after not only his wife but his niece.

The word 'expected' suggests that at some point in the play Eddie will be surprised to discover that he is playing out an inevitable and tragic story driven by things he is powerless to stop. Look up a dictionary definition of 'destiny' and see if you agree this is what Eddie is facing as the play unfolds.

Rodolpho, just as Eddie said to Beatrice, is regarded as a joker. Unlike Eddie, however, they seem to quite like this aspect of Rodolpho.

Rodolpho and Catherine return home. Eddie is relieved to learn they only went to a local cinema, not into New York's city centre. Rodolpho says he would like to leave the neighbourhood just once to see the bright lights he has dreamt of since he was a child.

Rodolpho is keen to be friends with Eddie and to show that he respects him for giving him shelter. Sensing that Eddie wants to talk with Catherine, he says he will go for a walk by the river.

Pause for thought

What do you think Eddie is feeling when Louis and Mike talk about Rodolpho to him?

Alamy

The bright lights of Manhattan seen across Brooklyn Bridge. What might this view of the bridge represent to characters in the play?

Key quotation

Them guys don't think of nobody but theirself! You marry him and the next time you see him it'll be for divorce! (Eddie, p. 41)

Eddie delivers a cruel message to Catherine. He tells her that Rodolpho is only being friendly to her so that he can marry her to get a passport and become an American citizen. Catherine is horrified. She loves Eddie and she now tells him that she loves Rodolpho. She is torn between these two feelings. She cannot understand why Eddie will not like Rodolpho and be happy for them. She runs into the house in tears.

Eddie storms off in a fury leaving Beatrice and Catherine alone. Driven and alarmed by Eddie's fury, Beatrice broaches what we suspect is a difficult subject for her. She tells Catherine that she is an attractive young woman but is still behaving like a little girl around Eddie. Beatrice wants her to act like a woman, not for example to walk around the house in her slip (underwear) or to go into the bathroom to talk to Eddie when

Pause for thought

What do you think might be Eddie's real reasons for not wanting Catherine to go to the city centre of New York with Rodolpho? Do you think Eddie is the sort of man who would regularly go there, or feel comfortable there?

he is shaving. Beatrice is careful not to let slip any hint that she might be jealous of Catherine for being able to make Eddie feel attracted to her. Just as Eddie's darker thoughts about Catherine can up to a point be convincingly dismissed as mere overprotectiveness, so Beatrice's potential jealousy towards the younger woman can be seen as sensible advice to a rather naive girl.

Beatrice sums up their conversation when she says (p. 44) 'you're a grown woman and you're in the same house with a grown man. So you'll act different now, heh?' Catherine promises that she will.

Grade *booster*

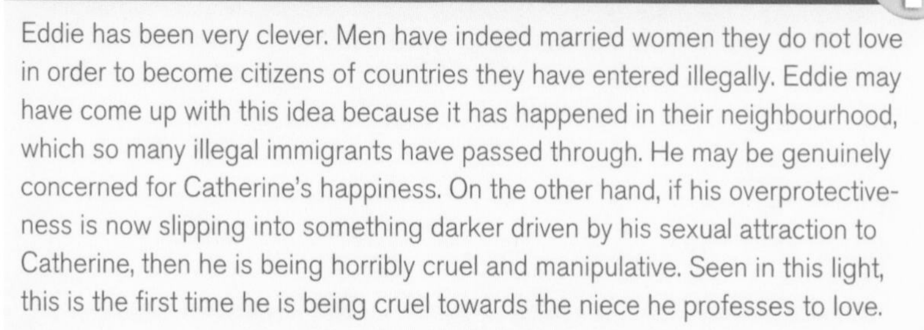

Eddie has been very clever. Men have indeed married women they do not love in order to become citizens of countries they have entered illegally. Eddie may have come up with this idea because it has happened in their neighbourhood, which so many illegal immigrants have passed through. He may be genuinely concerned for Catherine's happiness. On the other hand, if his overprotectiveness is now slipping into something darker driven by his sexual attraction to Catherine, then he is being horribly cruel and manipulative. Seen in this light, this is the first time he is being cruel towards the niece he professes to love.

You can use this section of the play to evidence how Eddie makes what appear to be reasonable points, based on knowledge that he claims to have which Beatrice and Catherine do not because they are women who stay at home. He appears to be offering good advice, when really he is trying to make people do what he wants regardless of the truth or their feelings.

Text focus

Even an apparently simple exchange has layers of meaning in a play as well written as *A View from the Bridge*. On p. 43, when Beatrice criticises Catherine for going into the bathroom to talk with Eddie, Miller shows that Catherine is an innocent and naive girl. First Catherine has to ask Beatrice when she did that — as if she has no recollection of it — and when Beatrice says 'I seen you in there this morning', Catherine says that she wanted to tell him something. She does not say what it was, so we assume it wasn't very important — it was the sort of thing that any sensible person would have waited to tell Eddie when he came out. Beatrice's use of 'I seen you' suggests that she was watching Catherine, that perhaps she has been watching Catherine around Eddie for some time because she suspects that Eddie has unnatural thoughts about his attractive and over-familiar niece, and that maybe Catherine, knowingly or not, recognises this and encourages it. If Beatrice has such suspicions she does not let Catherine see them here, and is keen to support Catherine to make up her seemingly confused mind about what she wants from her relationship with Rodolpho.

Eddie goes to see Alfieri in his office. This is the first time we see Alfieri talking 'naturally' to another character, as opposed to philosophically and directly to the audience. Eddie wants to know if there is any way he can stop Rodolpho marrying his niece. He says he believes Rodolpho is planning to marry purely to gain American citizenship. Eddie is showing a naive lack of understanding of the law; he may also be appealing on a human level to Alfieri not as a lawyer but as a kind of wise man in the community.

Eddie's stereotypical ideas about being a 'real man' are revealed to Alfieri when he talks about Rodolpho. He describes how Rodolpho has dressmaking skills, how he altered a dress for Catherine. Eddie and his friends are longshoremen — dockers — so we can imagine Eddie's horror at seeing Rodolpho's 'womanly' skills. When Eddie says 'I mean he looked so sweet there, like an angel — you could kiss him he was so sweet', we can imagine the contempt in his voice.

Alfieri tells Eddie he has no proof of Rodolpho's intentions and that anyway the law does not apply to such personal matters. Eddie persists and reveals the depth of his desperation to stop Catherine from marrying. He suggests that Rodolpho may be homosexual. Alfieri offers Eddie good 'man to man' advice. He sees that Eddie loves his niece too much — he is careful not to suggest anything darker in Eddie's feelings — and implores him to wish her luck and let her go. Almost in tears, Eddie leaves the office defeated, angry and frustrated.

Text focus

When (on p. 49) Alfieri asks what he is going to do now he has heard his advice, he triggers a passionate and tragic outburst from Eddie. Eddie reviews the hard life he has had, working to keep food on the table for Beatrice and Catherine. He says he has been a 'patsy', a simple person that others take advantage of. We see an admirable, honest man, but as the speech progresses the darker side of Eddie's passion breaks through. Miller writes the rather curious direction to the actor playing Eddie, '*It begins to break through*', suggesting that from this point Eddie can no longer keep the dark side of his passion hidden. He insults Rodolpho as a 'son-of-a-bitch punk'.

It is evening and all the main characters are finishing their dinner at the house. Catherine tells Eddie that Rodolpho has sailed from Italy to Africa helping out on fishing boats. Given what she knows Eddie thinks of Rodolpho, it is naive of her to do this. Eddie is unlikely to be impressed, and he isn't. There is general conversation about fish and about how oranges grow on trees back in Italy.

Key quotation

I could have finished the whole story that afternoon. It wasn't as though there was a mystery to unravel. I could see every step coming, step after step, like a dark figure walking down a hall towards a certain door.

(Alfieri, p. 50)

Pause for thought

Explain what Eddie means when he says 'I mean it might be a little more free here but it's just as strict' (p. 53). What is his motive for saying this?

Pause for thought

Eddie puts forward arguments that appear to be reasonable for not wanting Rodolpho and Catherine to go out so much, but in fact this is another example of Eddie manipulating people. What is his real reason for not wanting the pair to go out together?

Eddie is distracted, sullen and edgy. Beatrice is trying to keep the peace between the men. She asks Marco about his children. Marco is sad that he is away from them. Eddie, increasingly seeing both the cousins as enemies that he has allowed into his house, becomes unpleasant towards Marco. He suggests that when Marco goes home he might find his wife has more children (because she has been with other men). We can see that in the weeks and months (we are never told exactly how many) that the cousins have been staying, Eddie has become less and less friendly.

Grade ***booster***

It is a recurring device in the play for Alfieri to speak directly to the audience at key dramatic moments to show how Eddie's personal story is an example of a more universal human tragedy. After Eddie has left the office, Alfieri speaks of his growing foreboding of a tragedy that is approaching the Carbone family.

In a two-act play there is always a highly charged dramatic moment at the end of Act 1 that suggests great and climactic events yet to come. We might think that Eddie leaving Alfieri's office is the place to end Act 1. Miller, however, extends the Act further, adding Marco's humiliation of Eddie to the anger he already feels. This raises the dramatic tension and makes us even more fearful of what Eddie will be driven to do in Act 2.

Marco assures Eddie that he can trust his wife. Rodolpho supports this, saying that 'It's more strict in our town...It's not so free.' This remark angers Eddie, and everyone else is keen to agree with him to defuse the tense situation. Eddie says he thought both cousins were here to work not to enjoy themselves. He adopts a position of superior knowledge by saying that America may seem more free than Italy but there are still rules.

Eddie says that Catherine has been going out more and staying out later since Rodolpho has been in the house. Rodolpho is keen not to upset Eddie and tells him that he has respect for Catherine. This is an important concept in the society they have come from. Eddie conceals his dislike of Rodolpho's relationship with Catherine by making the apparently reasonable point that the more Rodolpho goes around town, the greater the risk of something happening that will get him noticed by the police.

Catherine again shows her naivety by asking Rodolpho to dance to a new record he has bought. This is only going make the situation worse. Rodolpho dances with her very reluctantly while Eddie glares at them. She asks Rodolpho about his time on the fishing boats again. He tells her he did the cooking for the crew. Eddie is horrified. It is another example (like the dressmaking) of Rodolpho's willingness to do what Eddie regards as 'women's work'. Everyone — except perhaps Catherine — is aware that Eddie is in a state of suppressed fury. Eddie suggests that he and Marco go to watch the boxing on Saturday. Marco is quiet, concerned about the atmosphere. Eddie tells Rodolpho he will teach him some simple boxing moves. Rodolpho does not want to do this but Eddie insists.

Eddie makes Rodolpho try to hit him, then lands a surprisingly hard blow on Rodolpho. Rodolpho challengingly puts the dance music on again. Marco ends the Act by asking Eddie if he can perform a test of strength: lift one of the dining chairs off the floor by holding one leg right at the bottom. Eddie cannot do it. Marco lifts the chair easily and holds it above his head. Eddie's authority has been challenged, his power has been lost. The image of Marco holding the chair high above everyone's head stays with the audience as the lights go down.

Key quotation

On p. 56 Beatrice offers one of the rare lines of praise she has for her husband in the whole play: 'Go ahead, Rodolpho. He's a good boxer, he could teach you.' Showing praise for her husband's ability to fight shows that Beatrice admires the kind of man that Eddie is.

Pause for thought

Look at all Marco's lines from the beginning of p. 54 to the end of Act 1. What does his contribution to the scene suggest about his mood?

Act 2

- Alfieri introduces Act 2.
- Catherine and Rodolpho are alone in the house. He takes her to the bedroom.
- Eddie arrives. He throws Rodolpho out. Catherine sides with Rodolpho. Eddie pays a second visit to Alfieri.
- Eddie phones the Immigration Bureau.
- The cousins have moved. Eddie and Beatrice argue about their marriage and about Catherine and Rodolpho marrying.
- Marco, Rodolpho and the Lipari brothers are arrested. Marco spits on Eddie. Everyone realises what Eddie has done and why.
- Alfieri bails Marco and Rodolpho. Rodolpho's marriage to Catherine is arranged to take place at once.

Photostgae

Actor Ivan Kaye as Marco lifts the chair at the end of Act 1 in the 1995 Strand Theatre production of the play. What is the importance of having a moment of high drama at the end of Act 1 in a two-act play?

- Beatrice and Catherine try to persuade Eddie to come to the wedding. Catherine turns against Eddie. Rodolpho tries to make peace with Eddie.
- Marco confronts Eddie in the street. They fight. Eddie dies.
- Alfieri talks of how he remembers Eddie.

Pause for thought

What does Alfieri's last comment on p. 59 — 'Catherine told me later that this was the first time they had been alone together in the house' — suggest about Alfieri's connection to the family and the events of the play?

What is the significance of Rodolpho and Catherine being alone in the way the story unfolds?

It is two days before Christmas. Rodolpho and Catherine are alone in the house for the first time.

Catherine is cutting out a dressmaking pattern. Rodolpho watches her closely. Catherine asks Rodolpho if he would still marry her if she wanted them to move back to Italy. She is testing him to see if Eddie's claim that he only wants to marry her in order to become an American citizen has any truth in it. Rodolpho says it would be terrible to have to go back to Italy. He insists the only reason he wants to be an American is so he can work legally and earn money for them both to have a good life.

Catherine becomes tearful when she imagines how angry Eddie will be when he learns they are going to marry. Rodolpho asks why she is so worried about what Eddie will feel and she gives a passionate speech

Grade *focus*

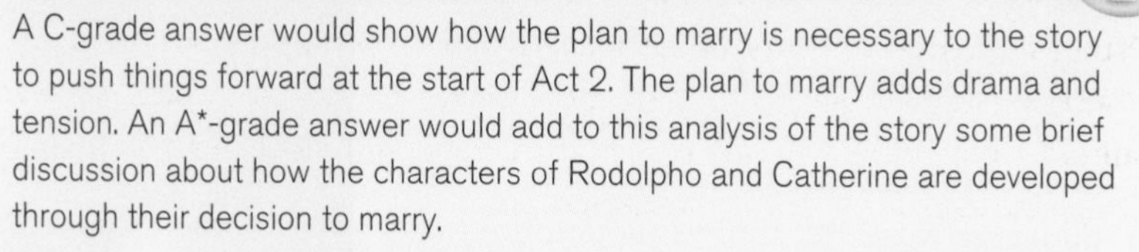

A C-grade answer would show how the plan to marry is necessary to the story to push things forward at the start of Act 2. The plan to marry adds drama and tension. An A*-grade answer would add to this analysis of the story some brief discussion about how the characters of Rodolpho and Catherine are developed through their decision to marry.

Both Catherine and Rodolpho are very young. We have not heard him propose marriage to her, yet the idea that this is what they will do has been growing since Beatrice and Catherine had their conversation on pp. 42–45. When Beatrice said 'Look, honey, you wanna get married, or don't you wanna get married?' (p. 42), this is the first time it has been actually suggested, but Catherine does not seem surprised by the suggestion.

Rodolpho could want to meet many American girls before settling down, and we get the impression that he is the only boyfriend Catherine has ever had. It may be that they love each other deeply, but it is also a sign of Rodolpho's desire to do the right thing in this society that he is ready to marry Catherine because he has shown his passion for her. His readiness to marry could be read as a sign that he respects both her and her family. Making this kind of general point about characters, supporting your own ideas with careful analysis of the text, will raise your grade.

(p. 62) about how she thinks Beatrice is not giving Eddie the love and support he needs. Catherine describes how she feels she has done that, always knowing how to do little things to make life a bit nicer for Eddie.

Rodolpho comforts Catherine; then he leads her off-stage towards the bedroom. We assume he has decided this is the moment they can make love for what we guess is the first time. Catherine seems willing for this to happen.

Pause for thought

Why do you think Catherine accuses Beatrice of not being 'a woman' for Eddie? Do you think she suspects that there are problems in Eddie and Beatrice's marriage? How does Rodolpho react to Catherine's concern for Eddie? Is there any suggestion that he thinks she is worrying too much?

Grade ***booster***

It is the combination of actions on stage and simple dialogue that creates the drama of the disappearance of Catherine and Rodolpho to the bedroom and the sudden unexpected appearance of Eddie, home early from work.

Catherine may merely want Rodolpho to comfort her but her line 'teach me, Rodolpho, hold me' (p. 63) can be read as an invitation for him to teach her about making love. Rodolpho has already been given the stage directions to watch her, to go close to her, suggesting he is aware this is a chance to be physical together. The moment they embrace and he leads her to the bedroom is the most passionate moment we have seen them share so far.

Pause for thought

Why do you think Miller creates a comic moment at a point where the drama is about to become much more violent and tragic?

When Eddie arrives there is a moment of physical comedy. He is drunk and removes, one at a time, whisky bottles from every pocket. Actors often play up Eddie's drunkenness by wandering about the stage, tossing their jacket towards the coat stand and missing, and so on.

Catherine comes out of the bedroom nervously adjusting her dress. When Rodolpho appears Eddie realises what has happened and orders Rodolpho to pack and go. In a moment where we see the power has now shifted from Eddie to Catherine and that she has sided with Rodolpho, Catherine says it is Eddie who should go.

Eddie responds by grabbing Catherine and kissing her on the mouth. Rodolpho dives at Eddie who pins his arms. He kisses Rodolpho on the mouth too. Drunkenness and his fury at losing Catherine to Rodolpho have made Eddie lose control. This is a climactic moment in the drama. Eddie cannot return to any normal relationship with either of them now. The play is accelerating towards its tragic conclusion.

Pause for thought

What has motivated Catherine to tell Eddie he should leave?

Do you think Catherine is being too cruel here?

The action of the play jumps over Christmas to 27 December, when a quieter, sober Eddie appears at Alfieri's office for a second time. He asks again for Alfieri's advice about stopping the marriage. Again Alfieri says there is no law against it. The new content in this second meeting is that Alfieri tells us that as he saw Eddie walking in through his doorway he knew that tragedy was now inevitable.

Pause for thought

Why does Eddie kiss Rodolpho on p. 64? What does this act reveal about Eddie's state of mind?

A phone box appears on stage. Usually it is lit in a single spotlight. Alfieri tells Eddie to let Catherine go, but then, as Eddie is leaving, it is as if Alfieri can see the phone box, can see that Eddie is going to betray the cousins to the Immigration Bureau. Eddie ignores Alfieri's plea and makes the fatal anonymous call.

From here on events conspire to make everything in Eddie's world collapse. He will do more harm than even he imagines he can do.

Text **focus**

You need to imagine how Eddie's call to the Immigration Bureau is played on stage and the effect that is created. The phone box is a lonely place, dimly lit. Eddie, who usually speaks his mind by asking questions and often repeating his thoughts, gives just the bare facts, then hangs up slowly when (we imagine) he is questioned for more details. He acts like a man who knows he is doing something terrible. He is at war with himself, but his desire to stop the marriage overcomes his natural sense of duty. He knows that he has potentially changed his life — and the lives of those he has betrayed — for ever.

TopFoto

How does the way this moment in the play is staged in this shot add to the atmosphere that Miller is trying to create around Eddie?

Eddie returns home. Beatrice is packing up the Christmas decorations. Marco and Rodolpho have moved to an apartment upstairs. Beatrice again asks Eddie why he has no sexual interest in her, but her complaint this time is more aggressive. It is as if events have changed things so much that she can let Eddie know she suspects he has too much erotic awareness of his niece. Eddie will not say what is wrong: he is the sort of man who could never easily explain sexual problems.

Beatrice tells Eddie that Catherine and Rodolpho are going to be married next week.

Catherine enters and tells Eddie he can come to the wedding if he wants to. She is very curt. Eddie tries one last time to persuade her not to get married. He is not hard or aggressive but Catherine barely notices: her mind is made up. When Eddie hears that there are two newly arrived illegal immigrants in the apartment with Marco and Rodolpho he suddenly panics. He becomes frantic, telling the women to get Marco and Rodolpho out of the house. Beatrice slowly realises what he must have done. The two new immigrants are relatives of neighbours.

Just as Beatrice is realising what Eddie's obsession with Catherine has driven him to do, the Immigration officers arrive. All the illegal immigrants are arrested. Marco spits in Eddie's face and tells him that he has killed his children: there is no way for him to make money to keep them alive in Italy.

If Eddie feels any remorse he does not show it. He shouts after Marco that he has to take back the insult.

Grade *focus*

A C-grade answer to a question about how Miller structures events to develop the drama in Act 2 would simply mention that bad timing causes Eddie to ruin the lives of two completely innocent new arrivals to New York.

An A*-grade answer would look to add some broader knowledge to this element of the play's story. 'Those whom the gods would destroy, they first make mad.' This ancient saying (no one knows who first used it) describes how in ancient Greek tragedy, events often combine in unexpected and cruel ways to bring more tribulations and disaster on tragic figures before their final death or destruction. A student producing A*-grade work should know that Miller was very interested in the devices of Greek tragedy at the time he was writing this play. Having two completely innocent men — Lipari the butcher's nephew and companion — ruined by Eddie's hatred of Marco and Rodolpho at the end of the play is the sort of awful twist of fate that destroys characters in ancient Greek plays.

Alfieri pays bail for the cousins, extracting a promise from a revenge-filled Marco that he will not try to hurt Eddie. This is the one time Alfieri fails to see the outcome of events. Rodolpho will still marry Catherine and be allowed to stay in America, but Marco will be deported in a few weeks.

The play moves forward to the wedding day. Eddie is refusing to attend. He has lost all standing and respect in the community because everyone suspects he informed on Beatrice's cousins. Rodolpho enters the room to collect Catherine. He wants to be friends with the man who is soon to be his close relation, almost like his father-in-law. He even tries to kiss Eddie's

Grade *booster*

We usually see Beatrice doing some sort of task in the house, making dinner, clearing the table etc. Here she is packing away the Christmas decorations. This subtly underlines the fact that the house is no longer a place of joy and happiness..

Pause for thought

Do you think Beatrice deliberately complains about her sexless marriage and tells Eddie that Catherine is going to be married? What might she be hoping to achieve? What is the significance (in terms of the power each character has) of Beatrice telling Eddie that the marriage has been arranged?

> **Pause for thought**
>
> In this brief meeting, Rodolpho is the one apologising for the way things have turned out. Do you think this is because he feels responsible because he is marrying Catherine, or might he know that Marco has resolved to kill Eddie and is on his way to the house?

hand but Eddie pulls it away. He suggests Eddie go out because he knows Marco is coming to the house looking for Eddie. Eddie refuses.

Marco appears in the street outside, calling for Eddie. Marco is mad with rage. Eddie is angry but much more articulate. He wants Marco to take back his accusation, although he is in fact guilty of informing, and morally guilty of betrayal in the eyes of the community. He wants his name back, and makes clear points about how he feels about the cousins. He says he has given them shelter at personal risk to his own family. He still claims Rodolpho only wants to marry Catherine to get a passport. He offers to forget the wrongs he believes have been done to him and make a fresh start: 'Now gimme my name and we go together to the wedding.'

> **Pause for thought**
>
> Do you think Eddie is really trying to make peace with Marco here?
>
> Does Eddie really believe Marco would ever go to the wedding with him?

TopFoto

Eddie threatens Rodolpho. What moment in the play does this still from a theatre production capture?

Eddie pushes things too far when he asks Marco to tell everyone what a liar he has been by accusing him of informing. Of course it is Eddie who is being untruthful. Marco is anyway too driven by rage to listen to any reason or excuse.

> **Pause for thought**
>
> To what extent, if at all, do you think that Catherine is the cause of Eddie's death? To what extent is Eddie the cause of his own death by confronting Marco armed with a knife?

Marco hits Eddie, sending him to the ground. When Eddie gets up, he has a knife in his hand. The men fight and Marco manages to turn the knife round and fatally stab Eddie. Catherine watches him dying in Beatrice's arms, crying that she has caused all this.

Review your learning

1. Why does the action of the play start on the day that it does?
2. What purpose does Eddie and Beatrice's telling of the story of Vinny Bolzano (pp. 23–24) serve in the structure of the play?
3. What things about Rodolpho does Eddie quickly come to dislike?
4. When Eddie speaks to Alfieri of his life and the way he feels about Rodolpho (p. 49) do you think Miller wants us to feel sympathy for him, even though he is on the verge of becoming a man with a dangerous and unnatural obsession? Why would Miller try to create these opposed reactions?
5. Explain the significance of Marco raising the chair at the point in the story where this occurs (p. 58).
6. Explain how Catherine and Eddie have changed between the end of Act 1 and the start of Act 2.
7. Do you think Alfieri was unwise to arrange for Marco to be allowed out of jail before his deportation?

(See answers on p. 85.)

More interactive questions and answers online.

Characterisation

- **Who are the characters?**
- **How do they relate to one another?**
- **What does each character want?**
- **Do they get what they want?**
- **How does Miller reveal the motives of characters to us?**
- **What evidence can we find to help us assess each character?**

Character map

Overview of characters' journeys through the play

Actors begin to build their understanding of a character they are to play by identifying:

- what situation their character is at the start of the drama
- the main motivation that drives them through the play, often called their 'journey'
- how their character's story is resolved and how they have been changed by events at the end of the play

This table will help you develop an overview of each character's journey through the play.

Character	Situation at start of play	Journey through play (main motivation)	Resolution of their journey
Eddie	Hard-working family man	Obsessed with desire for Catherine, hatred for Rodolpho	Killed by Marco
Beatrice	Loyal wife	Becomes angry and isolated from Eddie	United with Eddie as he dies
Catherine	Immature girl	Falls in love with Rodolpho, rejects Eddie	Sees she may have contributed to Eddie's death
Rodolpho	Eager immigrant, keen to become an American	Falls in love with Catherine	Will marry Catherine
Marco	Immigrant desperate to work to support family	He tries to keep quiet and work hard but is forced to challenge Eddie	Kills Eddie and will be executed for murder

Alfieri does not have a journey like the other characters because he is not fully part of their story. He principally observes and narrates, though he is part of three key scenes — two where he gives advice to Eddie and one where he arranges bail for the cousins. His journey is internal, in his thoughts. He says he prefers a world where people do not act violently out of honour and revenge, yet by the end of the play he finds himself remembering Eddie with 'love', as if he sees something in the dead man that, despite himself, he understands and maybe even recognises as part of his own inherited nature.

Pause for thought

What effect does the small size of the cast have on the atmosphere of the play? How does this tie into the fact that the play is set almost entirely in or around the Carbone house?

Eddie Carbone

Eddie is the main character in the play. All the other characters and the action of the plot revolve around him. He is the **protagonist**: what he wants drives the action of the play forward.

TopFoto

Eddie Carbone, played by Ken Stott in the 2009 production at the Duke of York's Theatre, London.

Pause for thought

If you were casting actors for *A View from the Bridge*, what physical qualities would you look for in the actor to play Eddie?

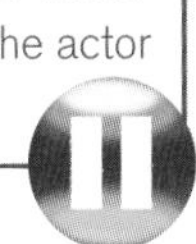

Grade *booster*

In most plays there will be a second character, the **antagonist**, who opposes what the protagonist wants and from this conflict the drama of the plot is created. In *A View from the Bridge*, what causes Eddie conflict and creates the drama is inside himself. Although Marco finally kills Eddie, he is not an antagonist who has opposed Eddie throughout the play. Until he challenges Eddie at the end of Act 1, Marco has in fact been the character in the play most like Eddie..

Within his world of work and family, Eddie is powerful, full of energy and driven by a sense of responsibility. He offers advice and tries to guide Catherine and, to a lesser extent, Beatrice. These are good and positive qualities. He is also forceful, dictatorial and, increasingly, obsessive, manipulative, self-deluding and self-interested. These are bad and negative qualities. The conflict between his good and bad qualities and the gradual rise of his bad ones is the force that drives the drama forward.

Of course, there is no clear divide between these qualities. Eddie being 'powerful' in the sense of having energy and opinions can easily slip into him becoming 'forceful' in the sense of being domineering and intolerant. It is the motivation behind what he says and the context within which he says it that determines when Eddie's good qualities become negative and destructive ones.

Examples of quotations (and explanations of them) that you might use in an exam to highlight these qualities follow.

Positive qualities

Powerful

'Now don't aggravate me, Katie, you are walkin' wavy!' (Eddie, p. 14)

Within four pages of the start of the play Eddie warns Catherine not to make him angry by contradicting him. This suggests that he has been — for good reasons or bad, we don't yet know — a strict guardian and that he is a man who does not like be contradicted in his own home.

Pause for thought

Eddie does not appear to have any interests outside the home and family. The only time we see him invited out — to go bowling with his workmates Louis and Mike (p. 67) — he turns them down to go home. If he had spent more time with friends how might this have changed the story the play tells?

Hard-working

'He was as good a man as he had to be in a life that was hard and even. He worked on the piers when there was work, he brought home his pay, and he lived.' (Alfieri, p. 26)

This key quotation in which Alfieri describes Eddie is full of information. Alfieri says several times in the play that Eddie was a good man because he was hard-working. That is enough to be considered good in the community Eddie lives in. He is not inventive, ambitious, brave or romantic, but he provides for his family. He takes work whenever he can get it, he brings the money home — he does not spend it on himself. Alfieri does not say he has a great life, that he saves or takes people out for exciting meals: he simply gets the money for himself and his family to live.

Full of energy

'I ain't startin' nothin', but I ain't gonna stand around lookin' at that. For that character I didn't bring her up.' (Eddie, p. 35)

Evidence of Eddie's energy comes across not so much in what he says but in how he says it. He has an opinion on everything that affects his family and on everyone else in the play. Here he makes clear to Beatrice that he considers he has the right to tell Catherine who she can become attracted to. Although even at this relatively early point in the play this is partly motivated by his secret desire to keep Catherine for himself, it shows that Eddie is used to exercising strict parental control.

Sense of responsibility towards his family

When Mike says to Eddie (p. 37) 'Believe me, Eddie, you got a lotta credit comin' to you', Eddie shrugs this praise off by saying 'Aah, they don't bother me, don't cost me nutt'n.' Mike's remark shows that Eddie is thought of as a good man, but Eddie just dismisses this. He is still partly motivated by what his community would see as a sense of duty and honour. In fact the cousins do potentially cost Eddie a lot: the house is crowded, Eddie is breaking the law and — we assume — the cousins don't pay much to Eddie for their accommodation. However, they are family and by helping them Eddie is merely doing what men like him are supposed to do.

> **Pause for thought**
>
> Where else in the play does Eddie cover up his desires to keep Catherine at home with what looks like good advice?

Offering advice

'You marry him and the next time you see him it'll be for divorce.' (Eddie, p. 41)

Although we increasingly come to realise that Eddie is trying to warn Catherine off Rodolpho for his own darker desires, it is still not unreasonable for Eddie to warn Catherine that Rodolpho could just want to marry to gain citizenship. Rodolpho is not like the hard-working, conventional, family men that Eddie knows, and Catherine is young and inexperienced. Eddie is her guardian and he wants to ensure she has the best life she can. At this stage in the play, and on first appearances, what Eddie says here might be seen as good advice.

Negative qualities

Forceful

'Ya can't tell, one a these days somebody's liable to step on his foot or sump'm. Come on, Rodolpho, I show you a couple a passes.' (Eddie, p. 56)

Eddie is encouraging, more or less forcing, Rodolpho to box with him. The subtext that motivates Eddie's enthusiasm for doing this is that he has just had to listen to Rodolpho's qualities listed by Catherine. Eddie cannot compete with these and though he would not want to be able to cook or sew like Rodolpho, Eddie feels driven to reassert his authority over the younger man who is taking centre stage in Catherine's eyes in Eddie's home, in his domain.

> **Pause for thought**
>
> Having called Rodolpho by his proper name here, why, just a few moments later (p. 57) does Eddie call him by his nickname 'Danish'? What do you think Rodolpho thinks about this name?

One thing that Eddie knows he can do that he is pretty sure Rodolpho cannot is fight. He conceals his real motive for gaining the upper hand over Rodolpho, for regaining pride of place in his own home, by saying that one day someone might put Rodolpho in a position where he has to fight. However, it is very unlikely that Rodolpho would fight if someone should slight him or as Eddie metaphorically puts it, 'step on his foot'.

Dictatorial

'No, you ain't goin' nowheres, he's the one.' (Eddie, p. 64)

Even though he is drunk, and Catherine has made her mind up to marry and become independent from Eddie, and even though Alfieri has warned Eddie to do nothing but give Catherine and Rodolpho his blessing, Eddie's suppressed passion for his niece combined with the authority he has naturally exercised over his family for years leads him to issue this automatic command. Catherine does not obey: this is the first time in the play his authority has been seriously challenged by her. This apparently simple moment is in fact a turning point for Eddie. It is a further dramatic step towards Catherine's increasing independence and Eddie's fate. Just two pages further on, Eddie will make his call to the Immigration authorities.

Text focus

Some of Eddie's attempts to control others can appear pretty desperate. On pp. 32–33 he stops Rodolpho singing: '[*indicating the rest of the building*]: Because we never had no singers here...all of a sudden there's a singer in the house, y'know what I mean?' In a large and probably noisy apartment block, hearing a man singing would hardly be likely to cause neighbours to investigate, and anyway most of them would most probably want to keep singing illegal immigrants hidden from the law! Eddie's warning does not have much logic to it. His real reason for saying it is to stop Rodolpho demonstrating a skill he has that Eddie hasn't and that Catherine finds attractive.

Obsessive

'Didn't you hear what I told you?' (Eddie, p. 66)

This apparently simple remark is the last line Eddie speaks to Alfieri and the only one in the scenes between the two men where (see the stage direction) Eddie is angry with Alfieri, a man he otherwise respects. Of course it is Eddie who is refusing to hear anything that is being said to him about letting Catherine go. He is so consumed by the dread of losing her that Alfieri can now see he is planning to do the worst thing he could do in this situation, regardless of the consequences to himself and anyone else.

Manipulative

Eddie's most obvious manipulation is his attempt to persuade Catherine that Rodolpho only wants to marry her to gain citizenship. But there are many other places through the play where he uses the affection or respect people have for him to make them do his bidding, or where he uses his experience of New York to prevent the cousins, especially Rodolpho, from doing what they want to do.

Self-deluding

'Tell the people, Marco, tell them what a liar you are!...Come on liar, you know what you done.' (Eddie, p. 84)

Marco has been honest throughout the play; it is too much for him to listen to Eddie saying that he has lied. Eddie and Marco are squaring up for a fight when Eddie says these lines and the atmosphere is so charged, Eddie's distress at Catherine being taken from him so overwhelming, that he appears to utterly believe that he is the injured party, not the cause of Marco's catastrophes.

Grade *focus*

If a question asked students to write about the key moments in Eddie's tragic story, a C-grade answer would list the key points in his growing obsession with Catherine and alienation from other characters, supporting each with a straight-forward quotation. An A*-grade answer would develop ideas about how the play is written using these quotations as starting points. An A*-grade student would point out that in a play, especially one like this written in simple everyday language, there is subtext under many lines: things the character is thinking or feeling but not expressing. Subtext is what gives a play depth, interest and meaning.

Self-interested

There is no single quotation that focuses on this driving force in Eddie's personality, because for much of the play he hides his desire to dominate situations by always having a reasonable explanation for making people do what he wants.

When things have reached crisis point for Eddie in Act 2, Beatrice adds to his panic about Catherine leaving by wanting him to talk about why they no longer have sex. Eddie says 'The last year or two I come in the house I don't know what's gonna hit me. It's a shootin' gallery in here and I'm the pigeon' (p. 69). Beatrice may make her point here quite aggressively, but it is reasonable for her to again ask Eddie to recognise the problem in their marriage that she has already raised in Act 1. The subject is too painful for Eddie to think about, so he turns the discussion into how bad things are for him in their relationship and ignores Beatrice's needs.

There is never any suggestion from anyone in the play that Eddie acts on his desires for Catherine; no suggestion that he has ever been abusive. Perhaps Eddie does not even acknowledge what his real feelings for her are and where they could lead. His confusion over what he feels — because the line between loving a child and wrongly desiring the adult that child becomes has been blurred in his mind — adds to his anger that drives the play towards its tragic climax.

Beatrice

Pause for thought

Apart from Eddie's repeated asking if he hasn't always done the best for Catherine, what evidence is there in the play that he and Beatrice have acted as good parents to Catherine?

'So I moved them out, what more do you want? You got your house now, you got your respect.' (Beatrice, p. 68)

Beatrice is a woman apparently driven by the needs of others in the play. She wants to keep a good and respectable house and to provide for her cousins. She wants to be a good wife and to be desired by Eddie as a wife again.

Grade *booster*

We never know why Eddie and Beatrice have no children, indeed it is never actually stated that they haven't. This is one of the many elements of character and relationships that Miller does not fill in. Deciding what we need to know about characters and about things that have happened in their lives before the play starts is one of the main creative decisions a playwright makes. Here, it is enough for us to know that Eddie and Beatrice have raised Catherine like the child they (almost certainly) never had.

Beatrice is nearly always seen engaged in some form of housework which contrasts — physically, in a stage production — with the fact that Eddie, home from work, is usually resting: sitting reading a paper, eating, maybe smoking. In many ways, Beatrice is simply the embodiment of a typical housewife ruled, not unkindly but continually and with authority, by her hard-working, money-providing husband.

Pause for thought

Why do you think Miller leaves details of their marriage up to now out of the play? What hints do we get of how they have worked as a couple to this point?

In fact, Beatrice has a strong personal motivation that drives the events of the play almost as much as Eddie's obsession with Catherine. She also provides a thread of reason that runs through the play.

While Eddie and later Marco compete for authority, while Rodolpho acts the fool or tries to impress Catherine without understanding that what he is doing will only annoy Eddie, and while Catherine shows her interest in and later affection for Rodolpho in front of Eddie without realising the effect this has on him, Beatrice is the one who tries to keep everyone calm. She tries to steer conversations away from points of potential dispute.

On pp. 34–35 she constantly tries to deflect Eddie's criticisms of Rodolpho. Finally (p. 35) when Beatrice sees how unreasonable Eddie's criticisms are ('And with that wacky hair; he's like a chorus girl or sump'm...I just hope that's his regular hair, that's all I hope') she shows another side of her character: her ability to stand up to Eddie when she needs to. She warns him 'Listen, you ain't gonna start nothin' here' and he backs down. Miller gives Eddie two telling line directions very quickly after this: [*He is already weakening*] and [*in retreat*]. These are telling the actor playing Eddie to quickly back down in the face of the criticism that Eddie knows is coming: his lack of sexual interest in his wife. In some areas and certainly in private, Beatrice has the power to challenge Eddie.

Beatrice has one key motivation, one thing she wants for herself that drives the play along, but she is quieter in putting forward her wishes than Eddie. She wants Catherine to get married, partly because she wants her to be happy but mainly so that the young woman will leave the home and be out of Eddie's sight and thoughts. Beatrice thinks this will help revive her sexless marriage.

Knowing Beatrice's mostly unspoken motivation — the subtext beneath many of her most important lines — allows us to analyse what she says to Catherine in more depth. The key scene between the two women is the conversation about how Catherine ought to behave around the house and whether she should marry Rodolpho (pp. 42–45).

'I told you fifty times already, you can't act the way you act.' (Beatrice, p. 43)

When Beatrice encourages Catherine to act in a more grown-up way around Eddie, this is good advice from an older woman to a less experienced one. Beatrice uses the idea that Catherine has not recognised her own adulthood to make the younger woman see her point of view. 'Like when he comes home sometimes you throw yourself at him like when you was twelve years old' (p. 43). Telling Catherine to act her age is the reasonable central point of Beatrice's advice.

'It's wonderful for a whole family to love each other, but you're a grown woman and you're in the same house with a grown man.' (p. 44)

Less obviously reasonable is the first reference to Catherine wanting to get married, which comes from Beatrice, not Catherine. If the younger woman is as naive and impressionable as she certainly seems to be, Beatrice might be putting an idea into Catherine's head. It would surely be more usual for the girl to tell the older woman she wants to marry, or has been asked by someone to marry; but by reversing the situation, Miller suggests that Beatrice is maybe the one driving things along at least partly for her own ends.

Text focus

Notice how Beatrice develops the idea of Catherine's acting younger than her age through their conversation. On p. 42 she says 'Don't tell me you don't know; you're not a baby any more'. On p. 43 she says '*you* think you're a baby'. On p. 44 Beatrice tells Catherine she is a grown woman and that if she does not marry Rodolpho she will end up an old maid. The effect of this constant reference to Catherine recognising her age is driving the conversation forward.

Grade ***booster***

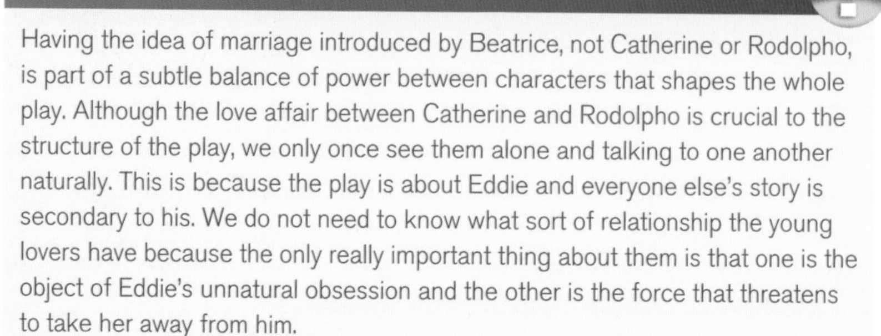

Having the idea of marriage introduced by Beatrice, not Catherine or Rodolpho, is part of a subtle balance of power between characters that shapes the whole play. Although the love affair between Catherine and Rodolpho is crucial to the structure of the play, we only once see them alone and talking to one another naturally. This is because the play is about Eddie and everyone else's story is secondary to his. We do not need to know what sort of relationship the young lovers have because the only really important thing about them is that one is the object of Eddie's unnatural obsession and the other is the force that threatens to take her away from him.

A C-grade student would identify this element of the story structure and note simply that the story revolves around Eddie so we do not need to see Rodolpho and Catherine alone creating their relationship. An A* student would explore possible further reasons for this omission: that by never seeing Rodolpho with Catherine we might suspect that he could be just using her to gain citizenship, that he may become more serious when he is with her, or that she may resist his advances and he seduce her, pulling her away from Eddie. Exploring ideas like this demonstrates that an A* student understands and can review the options a playwright balances when constructing a play.

Key quotation

You want somethin' else, Eddie, and you can never have her! (Beatrice, p. 83)

Key quotation

He was good to me, Rodolpho. You don't know him; he was always the sweetest guy to me. (Catherine, p. 62)

In Act 2, Beatrice finally realises that for Eddie to become a normal husband to her again she has to make him accept what he does not recognise is happening to him. She sees in him what he cannot see in himself. The anger she feels when he refuses to recognise that he is in the destructive grip of an obsession causes Beatrice to become angry with him, and this hastens the tragic ending of the play.

Her anger comes to a head on p. 83. This is the first and only time that Eddie appears to realise his true feelings for Catherine and confront his own madness — and it is the woman who, we realise in the last moments of the play, he loves more than anyone else in the world, who has to make him do this.

Pause for thought

Do you think that Eddie's sudden self-awareness influences his readiness to confront Marco and to have less regard for the outcome and his own life?

Catherine

Catherine's youth, naivety and apparent total innocence give her both charm and destructive power. She fails to understand the situation she is in with Eddie and that by acting younger than her age she is tempting Eddie to have unnatural desires for her. There is no suggestion that his obsession with her has ever been encouraged or even recognised by her, nonetheless it seems wilfully naive for her to — as Beatrice points out (p. 43) — walk about the house in her slip, or go into the bathroom when he is shaving.

Text focus

Catherine's explanation of why she went into the bathroom to see Eddie: 'Oh...well, I wanted to tell him something and I —' (p. 43) might just show that she is amazingly innocent, but the way it is punctuated, indicating a hesitation before she give her 'reason', shows she is thinking. Then she says 'Well I like to see him and I'm happy so I —' which again has an almost unbelievable naivety to it. Perhaps it is just that times have moved on in the fifty years since Miller created Catherine and we are all in some ways less innocent today, but to our ears Catherine seems perhaps just too innocent. Perhaps Miller is suggesting that Catherine is finding the fact that men find her attractive exciting. Now she is presenting herself just a bit to Eddie; probably without consciously realising what she is doing. He is the man she sees most in her daily life and seeing his reaction to her secretly pleases her.

TopFoto

Catherine (left, Hayley Atwell) and Beatrice (Mary Elizabeth Mastrantonio) in the 2009 production at the Duke of York's Theatre, London. What is Beatrice's attitude towards Catherine in this picture?

Catherine makes a big journey through the play. She begins as an inexperienced, rather wide-eyed girl who adores her uncle. Then she is attracted to Rodolpho to the extent that within a few weeks she is encouraged to marry him. By the last third of Act 2 she is furious with Eddie, turning against him with the same uncontrolled energy that she previously loved him with. Imagine the hurt Eddie must feel when she turns on him once she recognises that he has betrayed Rodolpho and Marco: 'He's a rat! He belongs in the sewer!...He bites people when they sleep! He comes when nobody's lookin' and poisons decent people.' (p. 81)

Pause for thought

On p. 43 Beatrice says to Catherine 'Was there ever any fella he liked for you?' Up to this point, had you assumed Rodolpho was the first boyfriend Catherine had ever had? What made you think this?

Text focus

Although Catherine's unrestrained tirade (pp. 80–81) against the man that up to a few weeks ago she adored is almost the last we hear from her in the play, there is a quieter moment towards the play's climax that suggests Catherine might be growing up, becoming more able to use reason and be less driven by simple and extreme emotions.

Catherine is present in the short interlude in the prison (pp. 77–80) when Alfieri offers to stand bail for Rodolpho and Marco. It is Catherine who has the longest speech in this scene, where she gives the reasons why Marco should promise not to seek revenge and salvage what he can from the dreadful situation. She also shifts her allegiance in this dispute away from Eddie. Her subtext is that she is trying to show Marco that by being ready to be Rodolpho's wife she is 'on their side' and against Eddie. The Catherine of Act 1 would not have taken such command of a highly dramatic situation.

Grade ***booster***

The lack of backstory for Catherine is another example of how Miller only provides the facts we need to know to understand Eddie's story. We do not even know what happened to Catherine's parents. The one thing we can infer is that Eddie has been a very good surrogate father because she loves him so much. Normally a young girl might be more attached to a female parental figure, but Catherine seems devoted to Eddie while her feelings for Beatrice are less developed in the play.

Pause for thought

Do you think Catherine is a weak character or a victim of circumstances that she could not be expected to understand?

Although *A View from the Bridge* is a play about Eddie and to that extent the other characters are a kind of supporting cast, we can regard the changes that Catherine goes through as a 'rites of passage' journey. This is a form of story where a character grows up through the duration of a play, facing challenges and overcoming them and growing to adulthood. Catherine's rites of passage is a tragic story: she becomes an aware adult, but her wedding, the celebration of her arrival to adulthood, is wiped out by the murder of the man that until recently she loved more than anyone else in the world.

Pause for thought

Do you think Catherine genuinely only realises what she has done at this last moment, or do you think she is so keen to follow her own desires that she recognises what might happen to Eddie but goes ahead and plans the marriage anyway?

Catherine's rites of passage development really begins at the start of Act 2. Here she has 'grown up' enough to question Rodolpho about his intentions in marrying her. Having been convinced by him that he loves her she is ready to give herself physically to him.

However, her journey into adulthood is a bitter one. Her anger with Eddie through most of Act 2 drives him more rapidly towards his death. At the very end of the play when she watches Eddie dying, Catherine finally seems to realise that she has some responsibility for his death when she says 'Eddie, I never meant to do nothing bad to you.' (p. 84) Her last line is full of new-found self-awareness, but also tragic remorse.

Rodolpho

Rodolpho is the more important of the two cousins. He is young, outgoing, amusing and very unlike Eddie, Marco or most of the other men that we imagine existing in the world of the play outside the scenes we actually see. His practical and creative talents could take him further than the hard manual labour of the docks, but like Marco he is indebted to the gang that have smuggled him to America. He could see himself as a victim in this situation, yet he never appears downhearted or unhappy, except when Catherine asks if he would still marry her if she insisted they returned to Italy. Even here, he addresses the situation positively: 'How can I bring you from a rich country to suffer in a poor country?' (p. 60)

> ***Key quotation***
>
> **RODOLPHO: [*laughing*] Oh, sure! It's a feature in our town. The horses in our town are skinnier than goats... [*He laughs*] In our town the horses are only for show. (p. 28)**

Rodolpho can sing, cook and even sew — all skills that Eddie would class as part of 'women's work'. We do not know how he acquired these skills or if he chose them from some creative urge — the important thing is that they show how unlike Eddie he is.

These skills, combined with his youth and outgoing, upbeat nature means he is instantly liked by Beatrice and of course Catherine. He comes into the world Eddie has created in the apartment like a breath of fresh air.

> ***Key quotation***
>
> **Me, I want to be an American. And then I want to go back to Italy when I am rich, and I will buy a motorcycle. (Rodolpho, p. 30)**

Unlike Marco, Rodolpho wants to remain in America and enjoy what it has to offer. During the course of Act 1 we learn that he buys clothes and records with his wages. He also takes Catherine out to the cinema. Unlike Marco, he has no one depending on him sending money home to Italy.

Rodolpho is respectful of Eddie and grateful for what Eddie has done for him and Marco. This respect would be expected in their society, so to that extent Rodolpho is merely obeying tradition. He has not however adopted the traditional values that a 'real man' is supposed to present to the world. Eddie reports to Beatrice that Rodolpho is a joker at work and regarded with a kind of amused scepticism by the other dockworkers. Perhaps Mike and Louis agree with Eddie's suspicion of Rodolpho in this role: 'Well he ain't exackly funny, but he's always like makin' remarks like, y'know?' (Mike, p. 37) Read in this way, we can infer that like Eddie they do not really understand Rodolpho or seem to want to befriend him. On the other hand, it could be that they like Rodolpho but just do not quite know how he makes everyone laugh. They certainly laugh at the memory of things he has done when working with them, which makes Eddie, as the stage direction indicates, troubled.

> ***Key quotation***
>
> **You never can remember what he says, y'know? But it's the way he says it. I mean he gives you a look sometimes and you start laughin'! (Mike, p. 38)**

Pause for thought

Even in a culture that demands the young respect the old, Rodolpho might sound too apologetic, too desperate to appease Eddie. What could be Rodolpho's motive in doing this, what subtext could underlie his conversation with Eddie on p. 82?

Even after Eddie has betrayed him and his brother, Rodolpho tries to do the right thing by the code of honour that Eddie lives by. He goes to Eddie and apologises for arranging to marry Catherine without asking his permission. Rodolpho thinks it is only this that has driven Eddie to betray the cousins. But he stands his own ground too, pointing out 'But you have insult me too. Maybe God understand why you did that to me. Maybe you did not mean to insult me at all —' (p. 82)

Notice how Rodolpho and his older brother appear to swap roles as the play progresses. To begin with Marco is the stronger, more sensible one: he wants to work in America for several years sending money home, then return to his family. He makes much less impact on the Carbone household than Rodolpho.

Yet by the end of the play it is Rodolpho who is doing everything he can to make things right between Marco and Eddie, while his brother blindly follows the code of honour that demands revenge even though it will bring about his own doom.

Grade *focus*

You may be asked a question that requires you to comment on the similarities and differences between the cousins. A C-grade answer would focus on the two men as individuals, while an A*-grade answer would explore how Miller wrote characters who illustrate very different approaches of people who go to other countries to live and work.

Marco sees America as a place to make money. We do not know what he thinks about being there. He does not appear touched or changed by it: he behaves at the end of the play exactly as a wronged man in some remote Italian village might. In an A*-grade answer you would explore the wider point that Marco is the kind of immigrant who wants to return home one day. He is a temporary economic migrant.

Rodolpho wants to savour all that America offers. He paints comic pictures of life in Italy — pushing the taxi up the hill for tips — and fondly remembers some things about home, but he does not ever want to go back. He makes this point forcefully to Catherine at the start of Act 2. In an A*-grade answer you would explore the wider point that Rodolpho is the kind of immigrant who embraces the opportunities of a new start in a new country.

Marco

Marco is the character in the play who is in many ways most like Eddie, yet he ends up Eddie's killer. Although Eddie produces the knife, we suspect that Marco would not have been happy with anything other than a fatal outcome from their confrontation. Marco shows no remorse as he watches Eddie die because he thinks Eddie is a murderer who has condemned his children back in Italy to illness, hunger and death.

Marco is a mix of opposites. At the start of the play he is cautious, grateful and almost speaks only when spoken to. We never really know what Marco is thinking because, until the end of the play, he does not express his feelings. It is hard to find revealing quotations from Marco because he does not often express himself.

There are however clues to some things about Marco such as his authority over his younger brother. When Rodolpho is talking about how he once made money singing (pp. 31–32) he says they lived off the money for 'six months'. Marco corrects him 'Two months.' Then Marco brings Rodolpho, who is enjoying telling the story, down to earth by saying that he lost the job because 'He sang too loud.' When Catherine asks Rodolpho to sing, there is a telling stage direction for Rodolpho, who '*takes his stance after getting a nod of permission from* MARCO' (p. 32). In this highly ordered society, the younger brother must look to the authority of his older sibling.

If Marco is seen to be so much the leader because of his age, it is not surprising that after Eddie has punched Rodolpho, Marco challenges Eddie to lift the chair by the bottom of one leg. This is warning Eddie that if he attacks Rodolpho again Marco will defend his younger brother with what we know to be his considerable strength. (Mike and Eddie have commented on Marco's strength and stamina at work.) Once again, Marco stays quiet, using action to convey his warning.

Although Marco and Eddie share many characteristics — they both put providing for the family above everything else — and probably opinions, Miller never gives us a scene where we see them enjoying one another's company. This is partly because, almost from their arrival, Eddie is suspicious of Rodolpho and this puts Marco on his guard.

The lack of a relationship between Marco and Eddie is also because ultimately Marco is only needed in the story as the character who kills Eddie. The play is not about Marco so we do not need to know why he is so different from his younger brother, what he thinks about being in New York.

Marco becomes a totally different character after he is betrayed. He is utterly driven by a primitive lust for revenge upon Eddie. In prison, he tells Alfieri what the lawyer knows and fears: 'All the law is not in a book' (p. 79). It is a simple statement — Marco rarely speaks more than a few words at a time — but it sums up one of the themes of the play. From this point to the end of the play Marco says and does nothing but demand revenge.

Key quotation

The law? All the law is not in a book. (Marco, p. 79)

Key quotation

MARCO: [*as he is taken off, pointing back at* EDDIE] That one! He killed my children! That one stole the food from my children! (p. 77)

Key quotation

MIKE: That older one, boy, he's a regular bull...

EDDIE: Yeah, he's a strong guy, that guy. Their father was a regular giant, supposed to be. (Mike and Eddie describing Marco, p. 37)

Pause for thought

In the final pages of the play, Marco seems as obsessed with revenge as Eddie is with his desire for Catherine. What point might Miller be making about these men by making them appear so similar while enemies?

Text focus

Look at what Marco says when he is offered bail by Alfieri (pp. 77–80). Marco really does not understand why Eddie should not die for what he has done. He seems both lacking in knowledge and understanding compared to Alfieri, yet also convinced he has to uphold some almost primal law of retribution. When he sullenly agrees not to go after Eddie he appears ashamed, as if he is agreeing only to please Alfieri. Marco, like Eddie, appears to hold the lawyer in a position of respect. Marco appears a good man who has been wronged and simply does not understand why natural justice cannot be invoked to gain him revenge. Yet he also lies to Alfieri, because the first thing he does on his release is go to confront Eddie.

Alfieri

Key quotation

Most of the time now we settle for half and I like it better. (Alfieri, p. 85)

Alfieri is a lawyer who works in the neighbourhood where the Carbone family live. He describes his business at the start of the play. He deals with small legal cases involving ordinary people — 'compensation cases, evictions, family squabbles — the petty troubles of the poor' (p. 12). The fact that his wife and friends have warned him that he works with people who 'lack elegance, glamour' suggests that those who know Alfieri well feel he is not achieving his professional potential.

This is important because there is an underlying feeling that Alfieri, although not necessarily trusted by people in the neighbourhood, is regarded by them as being of a higher rank than them. The clearest indication of this is that Eddie goes to Alfieri for legal advice about Catherine marrying Rodolpho, and even when told there is no law that applies to such things he still seeks advice from the lawyer a second time.

Pause for thought

Why do you think Miller chooses a lawyer rather than a priest as the person to whom Eddie turns for help and advice and to express his feelings to?

Eddie feels able to share his feelings with Alfieri. In a Catholic society such as the one Eddie lives in, the priest is the usual person that people turn to for moral advice and to confess.

After his first speech we learn nothing more about Alfieri himself. Nor does he ever express his emotions or thoughts except in terms of how the tragedy that engulfs Eddie and the others makes him feel. To this extent he is a minor character, but he has another role that makes him crucial to the structure of the play and the telling of the story. He is a narrator. This role is similar to that of the chorus in the classical Greek tragedies that Miller was interested in when he was writing *A View from the Bridge*. In these ancient plays, the chorus would stand apart from the drama and comment upon what was happening to other characters.

A narrator is a figure who speaks directly to the audience, who stands outside the story and explains things that are happening on stage.

Playwrights are often wary of using a narrator because they prefer what happens between characters to convey everything about the story. A narrator talking directly to the audience slows down the dramatic action on stage. When Alfieri is talking directly to the audience — especially at the start and end of the play — nothing else can be happening on stage.

Grade **booster**

Like almost all narrators in plays, Alfieri does not want anything from anyone else in the story. Eddie wants respect and he wants Catherine, Beatrice wants Eddie to be a husband to her again, Marco wants to work; but Alfieri has no personal stake in the drama. The details we learn from him at the start of the play are not so much to develop him as a character as to set up the world of the play and his position in it..

Alfieri's role as narrator is one that no other character can fulfil: notice that whenever he speaks directly to the audience he uses the past tense. He is thinking back to what happened to Eddie Carbone and the others in the past. His speech at the start of the play about the feeling of timelessness he had when hearing about Eddie's 'case' refers to the key theme of justice and honour that Miller wanted to explore.

'And the thought comes that...another lawyer, quite differently dressed, heard the same complaint and sat there as powerless as I, and watched it run its bloody course.' (p. 12)

We hear Alfieri talking directly to the audience three times (pp. 11–13, 26, 33–34) before he speaks within the drama, to Eddie when he first visits the lawyer's office. When Alfieri is talking to the audience his tone is almost of a man reflecting on things to himself. He sounds more thoughtful and almost poetic than any of the other characters in the play. This is in contrast to how he speaks when we see him in the action of the play, in the two visits Eddie makes to his office and in the prison when he stands bail for the cousins. When talking with other characters he sounds different from them, speaking in a more educated way and using more formal language structures. Nonetheless, he still sounds like he is from the same city as them. See the *Style* section of this guide (pp. 59–60) for more on this.

A View from the Bridge is set in a particular time and place among a very specific immigrant community. Miller, however, wanted to explore much more universal and timeless themes and Alfieri's role as a narrator speaking directly to the audience helps him achieve this.

Pause for thought

Apart from having to find another person to stand bail for Marco and Rodolpho, the logical structure and content of the plot works without the presence of Alfieri. What is the importance of Alfieri's role for Eddie?

Review your learning

1. Describe the relationship between Catherine and Eddie at the start of the play. Then describe it just before Eddie's death.
2. Describe the relationship between Eddie and Alfieri.
3. Why is Beatrice so keen that Catherine marries Rodolpho?
4. Why is Eddie embarrassed by the things Mike and Louis tell him about Rodolpho and the things he does at work?
5. Why does Miller give Rodolpho so many skills in things that Eddie would regard as 'women's work'?
6. Why does Catherine ask Rodolpho if he would still marry her if she insisted they went and lived in Italy?
7. Do you think Eddie really believes Marco has come to apologise to him at the end of the play? Why might he think that?

(See answers on pp. 86–87.)

More interactive questions and answers online.

Themes

- **What is a theme?**
- **What are the key themes of A View from the Bridge?**
- **How are the themes related to each other?**
- **How are the themes tied to the motive and actions of the characters?**

A theme is an idea, belief or philosophy that a writer explores through the story he or she tells. Very few great books or plays are just stories designed to entertain us: almost all encourage us to think about 'big' ideas because these ideas are the themes that drive the plot forward. A theme gives a story set in a particular time and place a timeless and universal appeal because great themes are part of our human condition. Shakespeare's play *Macbeth,* for example, is over 400 years old and deals with events that are supposed to have happened nearly a thousand years ago, but the work's main theme — how power can corrupt those who have it and tempt them to do dreadful acts — is as relevant today as it was when the play was written.

So let's explore the key themes that lie behind the story of *A View from the Bridge.*

Justice and the law

Throughout the play, Miller explores the potentially good and bad points of the sort of honour-driven code that Eddie and Marco live by. Their hard work and commitment to family is admirable. Eddie risks the law for months by harbouring illegal immigrants. Yet when he feels his territory and his status within his family and community is threatened, he acts in a way that will bring destruction onto himself and his family. Marco travels across the Atlantic to find work to provide for his family, yet his unthinking desire for revenge on Eddie is completely self-destructive for himself and those who depend on him.

Eddie will not admit to Marco that he has betrayed him, and he carries a knife to (potentially at least) kill Marco. Marco would rather kill Eddie to gain revenge and face execution in America than go back to Italy and do what he can for his children.

Miller creates a series of tragic events that destroy the two most principled and hard-working but flawed characters. There is an inevitability

Pause for thought

Natural justice can be defined as what we instinctively feel are right or wrong actions, regardless of what the law says. Given the conclusion of the play, what do you think Miller ultimately feels and wants us to feel about the idea of 'natural justice' that goes beyond the law?

about the tragic outcome of conflicts between men who are blinded by pride, and this allows Alfieri to claim from the very start of the play that he can see clearly how things will turn out.

The words 'justice' and 'law' are frequently heard in the play. In Alfieri's opening speech, Miller sets up the idea that justice and the law are going to be important. The lawyer refers to law in both ancient and modern contexts: 'in Sicily, from where their fathers came, the law has not been a friendly idea since the Greeks were beaten...I only came here when I was twenty-five. In those days, Al Capone, the greatest Carthaginian of all, was learning his trade on these pavements, and Frankie Yale himself was cut precisely in half by a machine-gun on the corner of Union Street, two blocks away' (p. 12).

Text **focus**

The things Alfieri says about Eddie on p. 85 add a brilliant touch of ambiguity to the last moments of the play. We might expect Miller to either end the story with the death of its main character, or to have Alfieri conclude the play by simply stating that Eddie's death was a waste and that he should have not blindly pursued natural justice.

However, while saying he prefers it that most people do not behave like Eddie, Alfieri also says that he remembers Eddie fondly: 'I think I will love him more than all my sensible clients' (p. 85). Notice that Alfieri says 'will', as if he will not forget Eddie, and his affection for the dead man will grow as time passes. He also compares his 'love' (a powerful emotion to express in this context) for Eddie with 'all' his sensible clients, suggesting just how deeply and strongly he has been affected by the death. There must have been something in Eddie's drive and passion that has deeply touched the lawyer.

It is this recognition of the qualities that Eddie had and the degree to which they have affected him that causes Alfieri to say he mourns Eddie with 'alarm'. Alfieri is shocked by what Eddie's forceful personality has triggered in himself.

To Alfieri, justice is a very important concept and one that should be linked to what the law says is just and right. However, he recognises that sometimes the legal system is incapable of delivering the kind of natural justice that some people believe in and want. He is suggesting that we will come to see how Eddie and Marco could not understand why the law could not deliver the justice they wanted. Eddie cannot understand why there is no law to stop Catherine and Rodolpho marrying, and Marco cannot understand why Eddie should not be punished for betraying him and Rodolpho.

Alfieri tells us he believes that it is best to settle for half, better to rely on a legal system and accept what it offers even if you are only half satisfied.

The written law may not always act in favour of justice yet it is better to obey the law than to take the law into your own hands.

Alfieri reiterates this point at the end of the play: 'Most of the time now we settle for half and I like it better' (p. 85). Having shown us Eddie's tragic story, Alfieri decides that he values the law more than any form of natural justice.

A View from the Bridge encourages us to ask 'What is justice? What makes justice?' Both Eddie and Marco have strong ideas of what is just and are prepared to go to great lengths to see that justice is done. However, they mistake their own desires for justice. They do not recognise any higher principle of justice separate from their own feelings. They do not recognise the kind of justice in which they have to settle for things they do not want. This is what leads to conflict.

Pause for thought

Why do you think Alfieri tells Marco 'Only God makes justice' (p. 79) when he is offering to stand bail for him?

Corbis

An Italian shop in New York. How does Miller create a sense of a community apart from the rest of the city throughout the play?

Honour

Honour is very important to the male characters, with the exception of Rodolpho, who does not talk about honour.

Honour means far more to Eddie and Marco than the law. To be honourable is to be respected. If you do anything dishonourable, you lose respect. That is why Marco and Eddie are so keen to protect their names and get a 'just' conclusion for themselves, which is logically impossible. Possessing and protecting your honour is for them a key part of their identity and of being a man.

Pause for thought

Why do you think Rodolpho does not appear to be interested in or motivated by a sense of honour?

Pause for thought

Do you think Eddie feels Rodolpho has honour? If Eddie thinks Rodolpho is not bothered about being seen as honourable, how might that make Eddie feel towards the younger man?

In the world of the play, agreed and understood codes of honour bind families and the whole neighbourhood with a sense of community. The positive side of this is that everyone should look out for one another. To betray someone is the most dishonourable action imaginable.

References to the high value of honour recur throughout the play:

Eddie tells Beatrice 'It's an honour, B. I mean it,' (p. 17) when they discuss the imminent arrival of the cousins.

Alfieri warns Eddie that he will lose the respect of the neighbourhood if he betrays the brothers. 'You won't have a friend in the world, Eddie! Even those who understand will turn against you, even the ones who feel the same will despise you!' (p. 67) Alfieri is a lawyer, yet he understands the power of honour to the extent that he encourages Eddie to do something illegal by continuing to keep the brothers hidden.

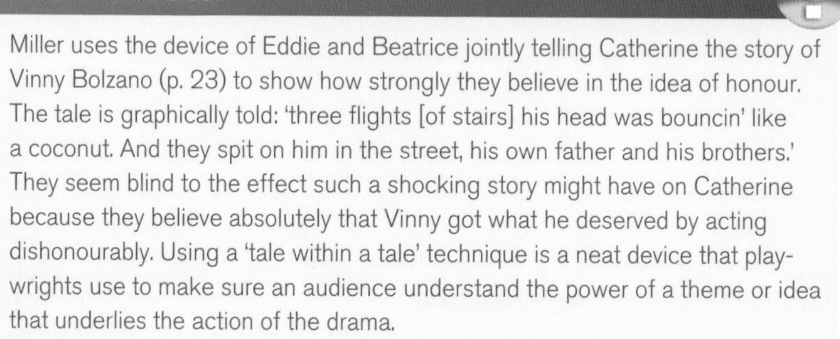

Grade ***booster***

Miller uses the device of Eddie and Beatrice jointly telling Catherine the story of Vinny Bolzano (p. 23) to show how strongly they believe in the idea of honour. The tale is graphically told: 'three flights [of stairs] his head was bouncin' like a coconut. And they spit on him in the street, his own father and his brothers.' They seem blind to the effect such a shocking story might have on Catherine because they believe absolutely that Vinny got what he deserved by acting dishonourably. Using a 'tale within a tale' technique is a neat device that playwrights use to make sure an audience understand the power of a theme or idea that underlies the action of the drama.

It is of course a dramatic irony that Eddie does just the same thing as Vinny.

Marco believes the only honourable course is to punish Eddie for betraying him and Rodolpho. Alfieri tries to persuade him not to pursue his desire for revenge: 'To promise not to kill is not dishonourable' (p. 78) but Marco's sense of honour is too strong. It blinds him to any logic.

Pause for thought

Do you think Eddie dies an 'honourable' death? He does not try to escape his fate — in fact, he encourages it — perhaps because he realises that to die might be better than to live with total dishonour.

At the end of the play, Eddie blindly refuses to believe that he has done anything wrong. He desperately wants his good name back after Marco's accusations cause the neighbourhood to turn away from Eddie. Miller does not make it clear if Eddie really believes that he has been wronged, in which case he is driven by a delusion; or if he knows he cannot admit what he has done and so desperately shouts that he is the injured party. No one actually says that the neighbourhood has turned against him. His claim to be the injured party could be summed up in the saying 'The best line of defence is attack.' For most people watching the play, however, the impression Eddie gives as he challenges Marco is of a desperate man who has lost any moral position.

Grade *booster*

Alfieri's oblique reference to people who might 'feel the same' as Eddie (p. 67) could just be a device by the lawyer to make Eddie feel less isolated in his secret passion for Catherine. It could also be a reference to there being people in their community who would recognise — and perhaps this is a new and growing thing for them — that to be good citizens they should obey the laws of the country they have come to live in rather than the codes of honour they have brought from their former homes.

Alfieri may also be trying to make Eddie feel that his reaction to Rodolpho coming into his house is something that other men in their community would understand and empathise with. Eddie is used to being in charge; now a young man has come into his house who has — perhaps unintentionally — challenged his authority over one of the women Eddie has looked after.

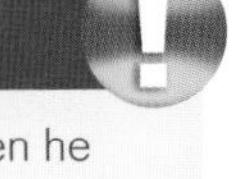

Grade *booster*

Notice that Marco gives Alfieri his word that he will not harm Eddie, then he immediately goes seeking revenge. In Marco's code of honour, it appears that the need for revenge is stronger than any fear about being dishonourable by breaking your word to someone who has just helped you.

Love

A View from the Bridge has none of the elements we would expect in any form of traditional love story. The love between Catherine and Rodolpho is only important insofar as it drives Eddie to fury. We can see this because Miller only gives us one scene where we see them alone together. Crucial steps in their growing passion — first date, first kiss, etc. — are not included in the play.

Although it is not a love story, the play explores various types of love. Different kinds of love are part of the motivation of almost all the characters. However, for many of them love causes pain and tragedy.

Love of a family

Beatrice, Eddie and Catherine are a loving family at the start of the play. Marco loves his family so much he has come to America to provide for them. Beatrice loves her family back in Sicily enough to support her cousins and take a risk by breaking the law for them.

Love between parents and children

Eddie loves Catherine deeply although they are actually uncle and niece. At the start of the play we see how this love has existed for a long time. However, Eddie's love for his niece becomes unnatural and destructive.

Love between brothers

Marco and Rodolpho have a strong bond — great enough for Marco to set out on a route of confrontation with Eddie by defending Rodolpho against Eddie's aggression. However, Marco's obsession with defending his — and by association his family's — honour causes his own destruction.

Love of place

Rodolpho and Marco speak very fondly of their homeland and to some extent appear to love it. Rodolpho loves America and the life it promises him.

Review your learning

1. Which of Miller's themes do you think is the most important one, and why?
2. Which of the play's themes do you think are particularly relevant to the world today?
3. Why do you think Miller was interested in the particular themes that the play explores? (Think about his personal experiences as well as his beliefs.)
4. Why do you think Miller chose to set the story of a man who had unnatural desires for his niece in a community like Red Hook?
5. How does Alfieri help us understand the themes of justice and the law? (Identify key places in the story.)

(See answers on p. 87.)

More interactive questions and answers online.

Style

- **What is the overall style of the play?**
- **What meanings should we look for in lines of dialogue?**
- **How does each main character speak?**
- **How does Miller create differences between each character's voice?**
- **How does Miller reveal characters' motives and feelings through what they say?**

Reading the play

A View from the Bridge is written in a naturalistic style. Miller wants us to imagine that — with the possible exception of Alfieri's longer speeches that open and close the play — we are listening to real people talking to each other as they would in their everyday lives. Although their conversations are often charged with great emotion, they do not have long speeches, because in real life people do not tend to speak at great length unless telling a story. Eddie, as suits the main character, has some longer speeches where he explains his feelings and actions: especially to Beatrice and Catherine, and to Alfieri on the two occasions he visits the lawyer.

Playwrights can only express themselves through the words they give their characters to speak. They cannot develop an authorial voice or a style like novelists, who speak directly to their readers. Some plays are written in a non-naturalistic style — in verse or in deliberately artificial, e.g. comic, language. However, the playwright does not have the same range of styles available as the novelist, who can 'paint pictures in words' of events and scenes; they can describe and analyse characters' inner lives, their thoughts and feelings.

Pause for thought

Look through the play and note some of the line directions that Miller gives. How do they help you 'hear' the play in your head? What examples can you give where a direction adds real meaning to your understanding of a line and the situation in which it is said?

Plays consist almost entirely of the lines the cast of actors speak. The only non-spoken parts in the text of a play are descriptions of the set, key lighting changes, stage directions to tell actors about any special moves, entrances and exits, etc; and line directions if a line has to be said in a particular way.

Novels can be of almost any length, but playwrights have to tell their stories in plays that can be performed in one evening, about two to three

hours. This means packing a lot into a relatively short text. To do this, playwrights try to make every line in a play do three things simultaneously:

- develop character
- advance the story
- deliver subtext

Even apparently simple dialogue can achieve all this if it is written by a good playwright. Miller was a great playwright, so let's see how this works with a simple exchange between Eddie and Alfieri from p. 45.

ALFIERI: ...there's nothing illegal about a girl falling in love with an immigrant.

EDDIE: Yeah, but what about it if the only reason for it is to get his papers?

ALFIERI: First of all you don't know that.

EDDIE: I see it in his eyes; he's laughin' at her and he's laughin' at me.

ALFIERI: Eddie, I'm a lawyer. I can only deal in what's provable. You understand that, don't you? Can you prove that?

Eddie's lines **develop his character** because they show us for the first time just how desperate he is to stop Rodolpho marrying Catherine. When he says that Rodolpho is laughing at him, this suggests Eddie feels threatened by Rodolpho. We glimpse the fury this is causing in Eddie. We see he is a man capable of letting that fury pour out.

His lines **develop the story** because we see how he reacts with emotion to Alfieri's reasoned and measured comments. This suggests that Eddie will react to events with emotions, not logic, if he feels threatened.

Finally, Eddie's lines convey the **subtext** that something more than Rodolpho's suitability as a husband for Catherine might be fuelling his anger. We do not at this stage know precisely what the source of this anger is, but we are beginning to suspect.

Alfieri's lines **develop his character** by showing us that, although we have up to now heard only his more reflective, poetic side, he has a logical mind. Each of his lines is a plain statement of fact made without any emotion. He asks Eddie questions, hoping to make Eddie come to understand for himself that he has no evidence to support his accusations against Rodolpho.

His lines **develop the story** because he states that Eddie can get no support from the law in his bid to stop the marriage. This lets us know that if Eddie is going to do anything he will have to act on his own.

There is **subtext** under what the lawyer says. Think back to his role as narrator at the start of the play when he said that throughout the story he felt powerless. He can only offer Eddie advice, not solutions. So in this extract when he twice asks Eddie if he can prove Rodolpho has bad intentions he is not really asking Eddie to come up with evidence: he is trying to make him see that he is going down a dangerous path and ought to stop now.

Any play is ultimately a script for actors to perform. It only reaches its full artistic potential and power when it is performed. Only then are all the subtle elements of what the playwright has written developed. A cast of actors and the director working on a production of *A View from the Bridge* would analyse in the lead-in to rehearsals every line of the play in the way we have just done for these five apparently simple speeches.

Miller's use of language

Miller wants us to believe everyone in the play is an 'ordinary' person, someone we could meet on the street. This is maybe harder for us to do than if the play was set in contemporary Britain because we are not tuned in to the New York way of speaking. Reading some exchanges between Eddie and Beatrice, for example, can make us think they are much more aggressive than they actually are. In real life, New Yorkers often sound brash and harsh to British ears. The use of rhetorical questions, something Eddie does a lot, can sound challenging to people not used to this form of conversation.

Pause for thought

If Miller is telling such an epic, timeless story, why do you think he chose to write it in everyday language instead of a more classically 'artistic', high-flown style?

In *A View from the Bridge* Miller subtly differentiates the way each character speaks. It has been said by some playwrights that in a good play the voices of the characters should be so well differentiated that you should be able to take any line out of context and know which character says it as much by the way it sounds as by the content. To help you understand the style of the play, let's look at the different voices of main characters.

Eddie

Eddie's very direct way of speaking makes his voice the most consistently forceful in the play. His language is raw and simple, reflecting a man used to having his own way in his home. It suits complaint, accusation and challenge more than affection, sympathy and subtle thought.

Eddie uses short sentences, each one usually containing only one thought, idea, request, complaint, etc. This appears to prevent him from developing his thoughts. The exception to this is in the first meeting with Alfieri where the force of his frustration drives him to make his longest speech in the play (p. 49). But even here, the basic crude energy that characterises his voice takes over, and the speech climaxes with his furious name-calling attack on Rodolpho: 'And now I gotta sit in my own house and look at a son-of-a-bitch punk like that…and he takes and puts his dirty filthy hands on her like a goddam thief.'

Eddie uses short lines to try and stop Beatrice's probing. He knows he has nothing to say about what is coming, so he tries to block off the flow of conversation. When he asks a question in the last line, he does not want an answer, he is using a rhetorical question to put a stop to the conversation.

Text focus

Eddie uses short, simple sentences to block conversations he does not want to have. The best example of this is when (pp. 35–36) Beatrice tries to confront Eddie about his lack of sexual interest in her.

'EDDIE:...I'm surprised at you; I sit there waitin' for you to wake up but everything is great with you.

BEATRICE: No, everything ain't great with me.

EDDIE: No?

BEATRICE: No. But I got other worries.

EDDIE: Yeah. [*He is already weakening.*]

BEATRICE: Yeah, you want me to tell you?

EDDIE [*in retreat*]: Why? What worries you got?

BEATRICE: When am I gonna be a wife again, Eddie?'

Grade ***booster***

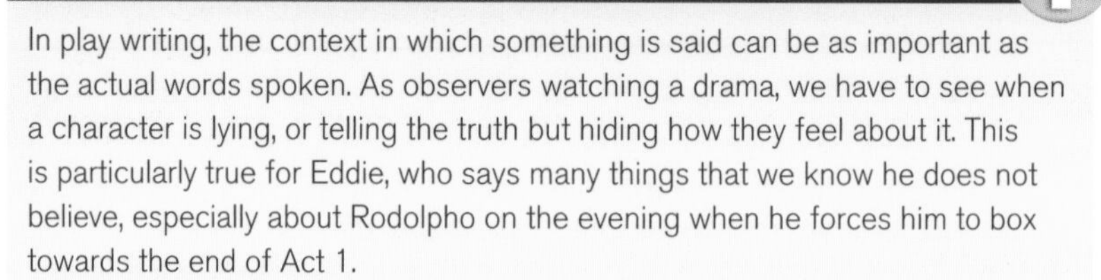

In play writing, the context in which something is said can be as important as the actual words spoken. As observers watching a drama, we have to see when a character is lying, or telling the truth but hiding how they feel about it. This is particularly true for Eddie, who says many things that we know he does not believe, especially about Rodolpho on the evening when he forces him to box towards the end of Act 1.

Pause for thought

Some playwrights do not try and convey the sound of a character's voice on the page. They write all the parts in ordinary English and leave the interpretation — the accents, etc. — to be developed by the actors when the script goes into production. Do you find Miller's use of devices to indicate how characters sound useful or confusing?

When this does not work, Eddie is forced to snap back at Beatrice with three blunt refusals to engage with her: 'I don't want to talk about it' then 'I can't talk about it' and finally 'I got nothin' to say about it!' Eddie is using the power of raw stubbornness to cut the conversation dead.

Miller wants Eddie to sound like a typical New York working man. The playwright made the decision to use devices like 'phonetic' respelling and running two words into one to convey in the text how Eddie should sound. This helps us hear his voice in our heads when reading the play.

Eddie's language does sometimes rise above the basic. He describes Catherine as walking wavy and says she is making men's heads turn like windmills. These moments add variety to the play and also a touch of humanity and comedy to Eddie's character.

Text focus

When Eddie talks to Beatrice about Rodolpho (pp. 34–35), beginning his criticism of the younger man by saying 'He gives me the heeby-jeebies', she is understandably confused about what he says. This passage of dialogue is a good example of how Miller uses **subtext** to add drama to the play.

Eddie is criticising Rodolpho for being effeminate, possibly even homosexual, something that we sense a man like Eddie would instinctively dislike. However, Eddie really dislikes the fact that Rodolpho is clearly attracted to Catherine, so in fact in this sense he is too heterosexual for Eddie. Eddie does not actually spell out either of these things as motivation for what he is saying, but we can see these contradictions are driving him.

Eddie's talk about Rodolpho's sexuality adds to his own discomfort when Beatrice steers their conversation at the end of p. 35 towards his lack of sexual interest in her.

Beatrice

Beatrice is the character in the play who sounds most like Eddie, probably because they have lived together for many years. She shares many of his ways of speaking that are typical of working-class New York and/or non-native speech, particularly the use of questions and reordering of the usual syntax of a sentence — so she will say 'All actresses they want to be around here' (p. 33) instead of the more grammatically conventional 'They all want to be actresses around here.'

She lacks some of her husband's aggressive edge; partly perhaps because she is a woman and certainly because she functions as a peacemaker in many scenes. Yet she can still speak both forcefully and persuasively when she feels it is necessary. When Catherine is attacking Eddie on p. 81, saying 'In the garbage he belongs!' Beatrice responds with a speech of short sharp statements, like verbal jabs: 'Then we all belong in the garbage. You, and me too. Don't say that. Whatever happened we all done it, and don't you ever forget it, Catherine.'

Text focus

On pp. 23–24, Eddie and Beatrice share the telling of the story of the boy who informed on his uncle. It is one of the few times in the play when they are not disagreeing. Miller is showing how both men and women in this community share the code of honour and the belief that it is right to punish those who break it, even to the extent of a father rejecting his own son.

Catherine

Catherine's voice also contains the Carbones' range of working-class New Yorkisms but there is, especially in Act 1, a consistent strain of girlish enthusiasm that makes her voice lighter and more upbeat. For example, 'They got oranges on the trees where he comes from, and lemons. Imagine —' (p. 39). We can imagine lines like this delivered by someone wide-eyed and smiling.

However, by the middle and end of Act 2, she is cursing people and demonstrating a kind of aggression (towards Eddie) in her speech similar to that expressed by Eddie himself. Her attacks on Eddie are particularly aggressive and stand in horrible contrast to the affectionate girl that she was in Act 1.

Rodolpho

Rodolpho's voice comes into the Carbone house like a breath of fresh air: a welcome one for Catherine and Beatrice at least. He is keen to show respect to his hosts but likes telling stories about his life: in Act 1 he describes his brief singing career, the job he sometimes engaged in back home of pushing the taxi up the hill, his dream of buying a motorcycle and carrying messages and, later, his voyages on fishing boats. Increasingly, his readiness to talk in a light-hearted way contrasts with Eddie's sullen fury and Marco's increasing silence.

Pause for thought

Do you think that Rodolpho's storytelling is driven by the same kind of natural enthusiasm that Catherine has for things in Act 1? Why would Miller want to give these two characters a stylistic link like this?

Rodolpho's grasp of English is not good and his language is often grammatically unlike that of native speakers of English and simply constructed, yet he clearly struggles to express his thoughts and feelings as well as he can. His story-telling and dreams for the future reveal an intelligent and active mind. He sounds like a man who would not try to be cunning or deceitful. This is in direct contrast to Eddie, who we increasingly realise is not revealing what he is really feeling even when he seems to be expressing simple thoughts.

Pause for thought

Do you think Rodolpho is simply angry with Catherine here, or at something more? What would this be?

Unlike Eddie, Rodolpho only becomes obviously angry once in the play, at the start of Act 2 when Catherine asks if he would still marry her if she wanted them to go and live in Italy. 'I am furious!...You think I would carry on my back the rest of my life a woman I didn't love just to be an American? It's so wonderful? You think we have no tall buildings in Italy? Electric lights? No wide streets? No flags? No automobiles? Only work we don't have' (p. 61).

Rodolpho's catalogue of things that exist both in America and Italy is both powerful and inventive. He says he is furious but he does not curse. His language, though comprised of short statements, is more imaginative and evocative than Eddie's when he is angry. This reflects Rodolpho's more creative and intelligent mind.

Marco

Marco has brought his sense of honour and justice directly from Italy and is driven by it without considering the consequences of his actions in this new country. To this extent, he has been completely untouched by his time in America.

He is the character we know the least about. We are given few details about his family back at home or about his former life. What we do know can be summed up as his motivation: he has to work to provide for his wife and children who are in desperate straits in a poverty-stricken country.

Marco appears to be naturally a man of few words. He rarely contributes more than one line at a time to conversations in the Carbone house. He may be doing this deliberately out of respect for Eddie, or for his own protection. He may suspect Eddie is less than honest with him.

Marco's habitual reserve makes his furious outbursts towards Eddie at the end of the play appear more shocking. Here he is like an animal baying for revenge. From what he says — and finally what he does — we suspect there is little analysis or thought going on in Marco. He is a simple man and he suffers for this.

Alfieri

Alfieri is not as much a part of the community that has shaped the other characters. His profession puts him beyond their daily lives. His speech reflects this: he has a more poetic and thoughtful tone when speaking to the audience as the narrator, and a quiet authority when talking with Eddie and later with Marco and Rodolpho.

Although he did not come to America until his early twenties, he believes he has left behind any sense of the value of the 'old Italian way' of settling disputes.

There is an air of quiet kindness behind much of what Alfieri says and does. He wants to help people. When he mentions the accident of a case of whisky being dropped while being unloaded just before Christmas (p. 59) — in fact stolen by the men and reported as lost overboard — this is a knowing remark about how dockers cheat the system in small ways. He does not disapprove.

He does not want to watch Eddie's tragedy unfold. He wishes Catherine and Rodolpho well with their plans to marry. Beyond this, he has no motive to drive him through the story. He does not want anything from any of the other characters.

Text focus

Alfieri's opening speech (pp. 11–13) is laid out in paragraphs which work just as they would in prose. Each one sets out a new idea in the speech.

The first two set up the world of the play for audiences who have never been to Red Hook. Alfieri begins in an easy, conversational way. He talks about the men he has just seen and the community in which he practises law. He makes a reference to the history of Sicily where many of the immigrants have come from.

In the third and fourth paragraphs Alfieri gives more details about himself and about the neighbourhood, particularly its violent recent history. He feels that people are becoming more 'Americanised' and he feels safer with this approach to life.

Alfieri's thoughts move beyond the law. He makes a subtle point about how unjust people can nonetheless commit just actions. This is the first reference to the play's theme of justice and law.

In the fifth paragraph Alfieri talks of how Eddie's case reminded him of the timelessness of the issues it raised. His speech becomes very poetic. He talks of the air in the office seeming to change, of imagining another lawyer from a distant period of history who had the same feeling hearing a case as Alfieri had when hearing Eddie. Alfieri vividly conveys his sense of being helpless to stop a tragedy that has been played out in many different versions through history..

Review your learning

1. Explain how Rodolpho's way of speaking is very different from Eddie's or Marco's.
2. What effect does Miller create by making Alfieri speak directly to the audience? (Think about how the playwright needs to engage the audience with the performance.)
3. Do you think that if Eddie had had the words to express himself better he might not have become so obsessed? Find places in the play where he seems to be struggling to express himself.
4. How does Miller try to convey on the page the way the play should sound when performed?

(See answers on pp. 87–88.)

More interactive questions and answers online.

Tackling the assessments

- How do you understand an exam question?
- How should you plan your answer?
- How do you plan your essay?
- How should you use quotations in an essay?
- How do you read an exam question thoroughly?
- What is the difference between foundation- and higher-tier exam questions?
- How can you improve your grade from C to A*?

Understanding an exam question

If you feel under pressure in the exam, the temptation is to read the question quickly and start writing. This is a mistake! Always read the question very carefully. Break it down until you understand exactly what it is asking you to write about. Be sure before you write a word that you are setting out to answer the question that is being asked, not just writing about things you have prepared. A good technique is to underline key words in the question.

Here is a higher-tier question, with key words underlined.

> 'All drama is about conflict.' Explore the main conflicts in the play to illustrate the truth of this saying about play writing. (OCR-type question)

'Explore' is asking you to identify the main conflicts between characters in the play and describe how they affect the story. You have to look beyond the main conflict between Eddie and Marco that leads to the play's climax.

'Conflict' does not mean a fight or even a disagreement: in a play a conflict can be a difference of motive or interest between characters that leads to them wanting different things. A character can also have an internal conflict. Clearly, Eddie is a man in conflict with himself and this should be part of your answer. Catherine too is torn between love for Rodolpho and love for Eddie, so she too is in conflict with herself. None of the other characters display internal conflict.

Grade *focus*

A C-grade answer might identify Catherine's conflict but not develop ideas about Eddie's internal struggle between his sense of duty towards his niece and his unnatural desire for her. An A* student would explore the conflicts in both characters. They would also point out that Catherine does not see Eddie's internal conflict.

'Illustrate' is asking you to provide good examples of conflicts in the play with detailed explanations of how Miller has created them and how they drive the drama of the story forward.

Planning your answer

The quickest way to plan an essay in an exam is to make a list of the key points you need to cover in the most logical sequence, or to plot these key points in a mind map or flow chart. Use whatever works best for you, but be sure to take a few minutes before you start writing to identify and note all the key points you need to answer the question.

You will have been given advice by your English teacher on how to plan an essay and you will have made sample plans, so this section will just remind you of key points about good essay structure.

It is crucial that the ideas you explore in your essay answer the question — and to make sure they do, you must read the question carefully and be clear what it is asking you to write about.

A good plan lays out exactly what you need to put into the essay and in what sequence. It will ensure you maintain a clear line of argument through the essay. If, for example, you are writing about how Eddie's obsession with Catherine gradually changes his personality and behaviour, you would generally make your points and choose your supporting quotations starting at the beginning of the play and working through to the end. If you dodge about the play, picking a quotation from end of Act 2, then going back to Act 1 etc., the essay is likely to be jumbled and your analysis of Eddie's journey through the story will be hard to follow. (There are exceptions to this 'start at the beginning' rule however: some questions may require you to build an argument by arranging key evidence from different parts of the text.)

The easiest structure for your essay plan is in three sections: beginning (introduction), middle (development) and end (conclusion).

The middle or main body of the essay is where you develop in detail the ideas you mentioned in your introduction: using quotations as evidence for your ideas, providing explanations for them and developing your personal opinions with close reference to the play.

The end or conclusion of an essay is where you sum up the main ideas you have been exploring. You must not just repeat the introduction though; you need to add some extra piece of information — possibly a quotation or some opinion of your own about the play — to further underline your main idea.

Grade **booster**

Do not wait until you have written to the end of your essay before you decide what additional idea, piece of information or quotation you are going to add to the conclusion. Your essay should build your thoughts to this conclusion, so you should know at the planning stage what is going to go into the final paragraph.

Here are some general hints for the three sections for an answer to the question about conflicts in the play (p. 61).

Beginning (introduction)

Keep the introduction short and simple. Refer to the question and give your initial response to it: that there is one overall conflict between Eddie and Marco that drives the drama of the play, but also several other conflicts that develop the tension of the story. Explain in no more than a couple of lines how you intend to answer the question: by working through the flow of events in the play showing how conflicts build around Eddie, or by taking each major relationship between Eddie and other characters and showing how the pressure on him mounts.

It would be important to point out in the introduction that all the conflicts involve Eddie: everyone else seems to get on pretty well! If you were making a mind map as your essay plan, Eddie would be at the centre and the other characters linked to him by branches detailing how they come into conflict with him.

You would also need to say that you will explore Eddie's internal conflict, and the conflict Catherine struggles with over loving — in different ways — both Eddie and Rodolpho.

Grade **booster**

If you can see the play as a story, a sequence of linked events, driven by what each of the main characters wants, then you can talk about the plot and the motives of the characters, showing you understand the two main principles that underlie play writing.

Middle (development)

If you have made a good plan, this part of your essay, though the longest, is the easiest to write because you know exactly what you need to say and in what order. The biggest challenge is to make it flow smoothly from point to point and to select the best quotations to illustrate your ideas.

If your sequence of key points is well planned then the essay will have an overall sense of flowing naturally from one point to the next.

Think about linking phrases you could use to construct your answer, for example:

This point is further illustrated/reinforced/highlighted/explored by...

Elsewhere in the play we see...

Another way in which Miller shows...

You will start an essay about conflicts in the play by describing how the conflict between Eddie and Marco is the main driving force through the play to the fatal conclusion, but also mention that to begin with there is no conflict between the men: it is Eddie's dislike of what is happening between Rodolpho and Catherine that pushes Marco to take Rodolpho's side against Eddie's increasingly unreasonable and aggressive behaviour at the end of Act 1.

When you move on to discuss how *internal* conflict adds to the drama of the play, you only have to deal with the conflicts in Eddie and Catherine. Neither speaks too often about how they are feeling torn between emotions and feelings of duty, but when they do — Eddie to Alfieri and Catherine to Beatrice — these are very powerful and dramatic moments which you will need to describe, supported by quotations.

Finally you need to describe the conflict between Eddie and Beatrice over his lack of sexual interest in her and show how this adds to the pressure he feels he is living under.

Grade **booster**

Always try to show you understand why characters are saying and doing things in the play. Imagine them as real people with thoughts and feelings. Try to see key events that you are writing about from each participating character's point of view — Eddie's frustration at discovering from Alfieri that there are no laws to stop Catherine and Rodolpho marrying, for example. This will help you see each character's motivation in a particular scene.

End (conclusion)

This is where you draw your arguments together, summing up how Miller uses conflict between and within characters to create the drama of the play. You should not however just repeat what you said in the introduction. You should find an additional idea to add to the conclusion, one that builds on the ideas you have explored in your development. In answering the question about conflict, this could be that the apparent lack of conflict between other characters makes Eddie feel more isolated because he feels he is the only one in the house who does not like the way things are developing. You might say how your analysis of the structure of the story and of characters shows that Eddie feels attacked from all sides: Beatrice is complaining about his lack of performance in bed, Catherine is more affectionate towards Rodolpho than him and Alfieri says there is no law to stop the marriage and he sees Eddie's secret desire for Catherine.

As well as adding an additional piece of information, you can also conclude with a well-chosen quotation. You might end this essay by saying that:

Eddie's fate was perhaps — as Alfieri suggests — always sealed because of the degree to which Eddie respected those who step up and fight in a conflict.

You would show this side of Eddie's nature by using the quotation from p. 66, when he is talking to Alfieri for the second time and he says with admiration for the smallest and weakest of natural creatures: 'if you catch a teeny mouse and you hold it in your hand, that mouse can give you the right kind of fight'.

Using quotations

Using quotations to evidence your argument and opinions is one of the most important elements of writing an exam essay. You will have the play with you in the exam, so you do not have to learn important quotations off by heart. The key skill is identifying the quotations that best support what you are saying in your essay. You have to know the whole play well to be able to do this.

You must comment on every quotation you use, saying what idea you are supporting with it. Your comment should never just be the quotation rewritten in your own words. When writing about a play, you have the opportunity to explore the subtext in a quotation: what the character means but isn't actually saying, or what emotion is motivating them but is not apparent in the line. For example, just after Eddie lands a punch on Rodolpho he rubs his fists together and says 'He could be very good, Marco. I'll teach him again'. (p. 57) Your comment on this quotation should explore the fact that everyone in the room knows that Rodolpho is no fighter and that Eddie is making a veiled threat that he will hit him again. Eddie is full of anger towards Rodolpho but not actually expressing it. By saying this line to Marco, who has not actually spoken for nearly a page, Eddie is also challenging Marco who he feels would always be on Rodolpho's side in any argument.

Pause for thought

Theatre companies often use one key quotation from a character in their publicity to sum up the motive that drives the character and creates drama. Find one key quotation that could make us interested in: Eddie, Catherine, Alfieri and Marco.

When you use quotations like this to explore both character and the author's style, you are showing the examiner that you have a deep understanding of the text. You are not just including quotations to show you have read the play!

Time is always limited in an exam and there is no point wasting it writing long quotations that do not develop your ideas or that you only make simple comments about. You could make a list of key quotations or mark them in your copy of the play so you can find what you want quickly when developing an idea in an exam essay.

PEE — Point, Evidence, Explanation

This is a useful structure to help you focus your point-by-point analysis of the play and express your ideas in a clear and concise way, using quotations to support what you are saying.

Start by identifying the point you want to make (within your overall essay plan). Then look for evidence and a quotation to support it from the relevant part of the play. Finally, explain how the evidence supports your point.

You might be writing an essay exploring the fatal and unnatural attraction that grows in Eddie for Catherine. You would need to make the point that only Beatrice ever challenges Eddie about his desire in plain terms: it is just too shocking for anyone else to confront him with. Most people think Eddie is a good, hard-working man and they are embarrassed to even suggest to him he is sexually attracted to his niece.

Having made this point you need a quotation as evidence to support your idea. One of the best for this is on p. 48 when Eddie is visiting Alfieri and the lawyer says to him 'A man works hard, he brings up a child, sometimes it's a niece, sometimes even a daughter…there is too much love for the daughter, there is too much love for the niece. Do you understand what I'm saying to you?'

Now you need to explain in detail what is in the quotation that develops your idea. You must say how Alfieri knows that in a potentially violent and strongly religious community such as he and Eddie live in, suggesting to a man that he may have sexual thoughts for a girl he has brought up like a daughter is a powerful and dangerous accusation. Therefore, Alfieri makes his advice like a general point, not a personal comment. Alfieri may also be, like most of the other characters, not quite ready to believe that a family man like Eddie could have such feelings.

Miller starts this quotation with Alfieri saying how a man works hard to support a family, something that Eddie is praised for doing several times in the play. Alfieri is implying praise for doing this. He ends the quotation by asking Eddie if he understands what he is saying: he wants to make sure Eddie understands that the 'general point' applies specifically to him. Alfieri knows, or perhaps just hopes, that Eddie has not yet fully realised what he is beginning to feel, and that this speech might shock him into self-awareness and end the dangerous situation.

Sample essay questions

When you read an essay title in an exam, you should first think about the key points you need to know about the play to be able to answer it. Remember that similar information and analysis can be used in different ways to answer different questions. You do not need a whole new body of information for every new question you tackle, but you do need to know exactly how to use your knowledge of the play in the right way to properly answer each question.

For example, if you are answering a question about how the play explores what happens when codes of behaviour and honour are broken, you should mention the key point that Eddie breaks two rules within the code of natural justice: not to betray the cousins, and not to abuse the trust Catherine has placed in him by becoming sexually aroused towards her.

If you were tackling a different question about the relationship between Eddie and Catherine you would also need to mention that Catherine recognises Eddie is — or has always been up to now — a good and honourable man in his community and a loving guardian to her. The recognition by her at the end of the play that he has betrayed both the community's code of justice and her trust in him needs you to refer to some of the same ideas you used in the first question, but to use them in a different way to create a high-scoring answer.

Here are sample essay titles with suggestions for key points you would need to include in a good answer. Take a moment to think in more detail about how you would answer each question. It would be good practice for the exam to make a simple plan of each answer.

Describe Eddie's idea of how a man should behave. Does his idea of manliness contribute to his death?

Key points

People regard Eddie as a good family man. He has raised his niece like a daughter and he is ready to risk the law to take in the cousins. Eddie likes to think of himself as an ordinary, hard-working man.

Catherine refers to how she can tell when he is tired. We do not know how old Eddie is but he is not a young man and he does a hard physical job. Maybe awareness of his declining strength makes him more defensive and ready to prove himself.

Eddie finds Rodolpho effeminate and so not a real man. He does not like the fact that his workmates laugh at Rodolpho because this means they are laughing at someone in his family. He hates the fact that a man like Rodolpho could become Catherine's husband.

When Marco shames Eddie at the end of Act 1 the stakes are raised and Eddie needs to get his pride back. Although Eddie is not apparently a habitually violent man, he is happy to box with Rodolpho and we suspect he can fight if he has to.

Grade *booster*

If the meaning of a question seems unclear or too open to interpretation, consider choosing another question if there is a choice. If you still decide to tackle this question, make it clear what your interpretation of the question is.

Grade *booster*

Many two-part questions ask you to comment (a) on how a character is presented in the passage, then (b) how that character reflects a particular theme. Prepare for these by making sure you know which themes especially relate to each character.

Grade **booster**

If you were answering a question about how characters react to Rodolpho, you would gain marks if, as well as saying that Eddie might be uncomfortable (pp. 37–38) with Mike and Louis laughing about Rodolpho because he thinks they are laughing *at* him, you also said that maybe Eddie feels resentful that Rodolpho has found some connection with his workmates. Mike and Louis are laughing *with* Rodolpho (not *at* him) and Eddie cannot understand this.

It is not clear (to most audiences) if carrying a knife is a cowardly thing to do or something that people in that community might expect a man whose honour is being challenged to do. Marco does not have a knife; Eddie is killed when his own weapon is turned on him. Marco is the younger man so Eddie was maybe foolish to stand up to him, but Eddie's idea of being a man means he can't not step up to fight.

Describe the development of the relationship between Catherine and Rodolpho. Why does she find him attractive?

It would be best to approach this essay by first describing the things that make Rodolpho attractive to Catherine, then showing what sort of life she has had before meeting him. You should not try and chart their growing love week by week because Miller does not provide scenes where we see them alone except at the beginning of Act 2 when they are already planning to get married. We mainly see the development of their passion in terms of how it affects Eddie.

Key points

Rodolpho is very different from Eddie and most of the men Catherine would have met through him.

Rodolpho seems part of a new and younger generation. He wants to work hard like the others but also wants to have fun.

Rodolpho pays attention to things that interest Catherine, such as cooking and dressmaking, things that other men would regard as women's skills. But Rodolpho is not afraid to stand up for himself in his own way with men on the docks or with Eddie at home. He does not pretend to act tough to fit in.

He can take control of the situation between himself and Catherine. He leads her to the bedroom at the start of Act 2.

Catherine is 17 and just beginning to realise that men find her attractive.

Throughout Act 1 Catherine is constantly happily surprised by aspects of Rodolpho: his blond hair, his singing, his dressmaking and cooking skills and the fact he spends money on taking her out and on pleasures like buying records.

How does Miller explore the difference between the law and natural justice in the play?

Key points

Miller introduces the idea that natural justice and law are different things in Alfieri's speech at the start of the play.

Alfieri suggests that justice means different things to different people. He says that the community is becoming less driven to seek natural justice and that maybe this is a good thing.

Eddie and the community he lives in have no compunction about breaking the law by giving shelter to relatives who are illegal immigrants.

The idea that betrayal is the worst kind of injustice is explored through the retelling of the story of Vinny Bolzano.

Through Act 1 Eddie begins to feel he is being treated unjustly: first by Catherine and Rodolpho becoming attracted to one another, then by his wife complaining about the lack of sex in their marriage, and finally by Alfieiri telling him there is no law that can be used to stop Rodolpho and Catherine marrying.

Eddie's suppressed passion for Catherine makes him blind to the bad motives he begins to unfairly project onto other people: for example, suggesting to Catherine that Rodolpho only wants to marry her to gain citizenship.

Eddie's change of personality reaches its climax when he informs on the cousins to the Immigration Bureau.

Marco's desire for justice through revenge on Eddie drives the play towards its tragic climax.

Eddie's refusal to back down inflames the confrontation with Marco. Eddie is being completely false and unjust and pays the ultimate price.

Higher- and foundation-tier essays

Foundation tier

Foundation-tier questions are easier to answer than those for the higher tier. They might be based on discussing character rather than on themes or on analysis of the play's style for example. However, the highest grade you can get at foundation tier is a C.

The skills you need to develop to do well at either tier are the same, but if you know you are being entered for the foundation tier be careful not to do any of the things listed under the heading 'What you will not get marks for' at the end of the *Assessment objectives and skills* section of this guide.

Foundation-tier questions usually have a number of bullet point hints to help you plan your answer. Make sure you think carefully about these and use them as the basis of your essay plan.

Below are four examples of foundation-tier type questions. (These questions could be set by any of the exam boards.)

1 Beatrice and Catherine are the only women in the play. Describe how you imagine each of them feels about the cousins who come to stay. Consider:

- How Beatrice feels about Catherine's growing affection for Rodolpho.
- Why Beatrice encourages Catherine to marry Rodolpho and how she feels when she knows this is going to happen.
- What Catherine feels about both cousins — especially Rodolpho — when they first arrive.
- What happens to make the friendship between Catherine and Rodolpho develop into a love affair.
- What motivates them to agree to marry quite quickly.

2 Alfieri says that Eddie's death is useless. Explore what he means by this. You should think about:

- Alfieri's belief from the very start of the play that what happens to Eddie is just a modern version of an age-old story.
- His understanding that no law can prevent Catherine and Rodolpho marrying.
- Eddie's refusal to accept Rodolpho as just a different sort of man.
- Eddie's growing and unnatural desire for his niece that blinds him to other considerations.
- Marco's killing of Eddie which will lead — if he is convicted — to him dying as well because he will be sentenced to death.

3 How are ideas of behaving like a man and aggression combined in the play and what are the results? Consider:

- The tough lives men like Eddie and Marco have led in New York and Italy.
- The challenges they faced when they arrived in a new country.
- The traditional role in their society of men as the providers and leaders in their families.
- The tradition of personal pride and honour that men like them are supposed to uphold and, if necessary, fight to preserve.

4 Discuss the idea of how keeping secrets affects the way people act in the play. You should explain:

- Why Eddie and his family risk the law to hide the cousins.
- Why it is so hard for Eddie to admit even to himself that he is attracted to Catherine.

- The idea that Eddie 'confesses' some of his feelings to Alfieri, who he regards as some sort of 'wise man' as well as a lawyer.
- The extent to which Rodolpho and Catherine keep the seriousness of their love secret from Eddie until they decide to get married.

Higher tier

At higher tier you will not usually be given bullet points to help you plan your answer. However, they might be provided if it is considered a particularly demanding question. If they are, use them as the basis for your essay plan. If there are no bullet points, think carefully about exactly what information and ideas the question is asking you to write about. A question may ask you several different things: how to deal with this sort of question is discussed in the next section.

At higher-tier level you are more likely to be asked to write about the play's themes or style. This is especially true of questions set by the OCR exam board.

Here are four examples of higher-tier questions (OCR and WJEC boards).

1 At the start of the play Alfieri says 'Now we settle for half, and I like it better.' Discuss how not settling for half drives the action of the play. (OCR-style question)

2 Describe how Miller builds the sequence of events that creates the pressure on Eddie that drives him to make the fateful call to the immigration authorities. (OCR-style question)

3 How does Miller create the voices of Eddie and Beatrice? Use examples to explore the way they express themselves and describe how they sound to you. (WJEC-style question)

4 To what extent does Eddie uphold the law and rules of the society he is part of, and to what extent does he break them? (OCR- and WJEC-style question)

Pause for thought

As a revision exercise, go through the four higher-tier questions on these pages and suggest the bullet-point guidance you would expect to see if they were offered at the foundation tier. This is a useful activity whichever tier you are entered for.

You will see that higher-tier and foundation-tier questions are similar. The main difference is that foundation-tier candidates will receive guidance about how to tackle the question.

Improving your grade from C to A*

You can almost always make an improvement in your grade if you develop a clear understanding of three key areas that you need to consider when writing about a set text:

1 What is the writer aiming to do?
2 How do they go about doing it?
3 Have they been successful?

Many students focus too much on the second point and miss the others. They spend a lot of time just retelling the story in their own words. Obviously, you need to constantly refer to the text to make any important points but if your essay is mostly just retelling the story you are not going to get a good grade. The basic plot of *A View from the Bridge* is really quite simple: it is the way it is told, the way that characters are developed and how language is used to create their voices, that make it a great work.

Grade **booster**

A useful revision exercise to help you improve your grade is to:

- Write down in a notebook the key events of the play.
- Write a one-paragraph description of each of the major characters.
- Write a brief summary of what the writer set out to do.

You must give thought to the first point (the writer's aims) before planning or writing any essay. Make sure you understand what kind of play Miller wanted to create, what ideas he was interested in exploring. (See the *Context* section of this guide for more on this background information.)

Then you can start on the second point: how Miller set about achieving his aims for the play. Decide what you want to say about the play and identify the scenes and lines that will provide evidence for your ideas.

To gain a high grade you need to be able to make a judgement, supported by evidence, about whether you think Miller has achieved his aims. If you think Miller has successfully created believable, dynamic characters who dramatically play out a modern version of a classic tragedy, find evidence through the play to support your claim.

In addition, a high-grade answer will always contain well-expressed personal responses. How did events and characters in the play make you feel, and how was this effect achieved?

Here are the criteria that will be used by examiners to assess your written work. Look at the difference between what is needed to gain a C grade compared to an A*. Think about how you can meet the criteria for the higher grade in your study of, and response to, *A View from the Bridge*.

C-grade candidates

- Show understanding of how meanings and ideas are conveyed through language, structure and form.
- Show awareness of some of the cultural and social context of texts and convey ideas appropriately in a range of forms.

A-grade candidates

- Respond critically and sensitively to a range of texts, taking into account alternative approaches and interpretations.
- Explore and evaluate the way meanings, ideas and feelings are conveyed through language, structure and form, making comparisons and connections between texts.
- Identify and comment on social, historical and cultural contexts of texts, and show awareness of literary tradition.
- Select forms appropriately and convey ideas coherently.

Review your learning

1. Describe a good, mark-scoring way to use quotations in an exam essay.
2. Explain the PEE process for constructing exam answers.
3. How should you use the bullet points in a foundation-tier essay question?
4. What simple technique helps you understand a question which has no bullet points?
5. What three key areas do you need to consider when writing about a set text?

(See answers on p. 88.)

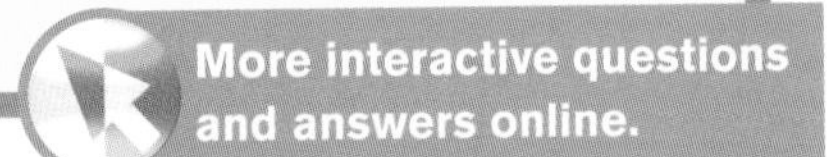

Assessment Objectives and skills

- How will your essay be marked?
- What are the Assessment Objectives?
- How do the Assessment Objectives apply to different exam boards?
- What skills are you required to show?
- How can you gain extra marks related to each Assessment Objective?
- Improving your grade
- Getting an A*

How will your essay be marked?

An examiner or moderator marking your work will be trying to reward you as far as possible, but will only be able to do so if you succeed in fulfilling the key Assessment Objectives for this section of your English Literature assessment.

Assessment Objectives

The Assessment Objectives that you will be assessed on are:

- **AO1** — Respond to texts critically and imaginatively; select and evaluate relevant textual detail to illustrate and support interpretations.
- **AO2** — Explain how language, structure and form contribute to writers' presentation of ideas, themes and settings.

Exam board summary

The table below summarises the percentage weighting for each Assessment Objective for the contemporary drama sections (including *A View from the Bridge*) for each of the exam boards that offer this text. They add up to different amounts because this section forms only one part of the overall assessment.

	AO1	AO2	AO3	Overall
WJEC (i)	3.33	3.33		
(ii) and (iii)	4.44	8.88		10%
Edexcel	10 On AVFTB you will only be assessed on AO1	5 Shakespeare	10 Shakespeare	25%
OCR	12.5	12.5		25%

WJEC

The contemporary drama questions appear on a two-hour examination paper that also tests your knowledge of Literary Heritage Prose. You should spend an hour on your drama questions. Question (i) asks for close analysis of a given passage from the play. You then have a choice of two further questions, (ii) and (iii), each of which relates to the play as a whole. The exam is closed text. This whole paper is worth 20% of your overall award, so your drama questions are worth half of this, as specified in the table above.

Edexcel

Edexcel assesses your knowledge of contemporary drama through controlled assessment, which includes two tasks, one on *A View from the Bridge* and another on a Shakespeare play. Your teacher selects your tasks from a choice given by the board. The tasks focus on character, theme, performance or relationships. Your modern drama tasks are marked out of 20 and the Shakespeare out of 30. Both tasks together are worth 25% of your overall award, as specified in the table above. You will be allowed access to an unannotated copy of *A View from the Bridge*, a dictionary or thesaurus, spell and grammar checks, and notes, provided they are not in continuous prose (i.e. complete paragraphs that you could simply copy out). You will not be allowed access to the internet, prepared materials on a hard drive or a first draft of your work for the task.

OCR

For OCR you are assessed in an examination of 45 minutes that is worth 25% of your overall qualification. You are asked one passage-based essay question on *A View from the Bridge*.

What skills do you need to show?

Let's break the Assessment Objectives down to see exactly what they mean.

AO1

Respond to texts **critically** and **imaginatively**; **select and evaluate relevant textual detail to illustrate and support interpretations**.

- **Respond to texts critically:** this means you must say what you think of the play and why. You are being asked to **evaluate** it. This involves realising that the author has made choices as he has constructed the play, and giving your views on how effective these choices are.
- **Respond to texts imaginatively:** this means your ideas need to be interesting and exploratory. You will need to see themes, ideas and settings in the play in an imaginative manner. You will need to come up with answers that explore the play and different potential meanings. You will need to understand there may be more than one interpretation of an idea or moment in the story.
- **select...relevant textual detail to illustrate and support interpretations:** this means giving short quotations from the play, to support your views. You will also need to be able to reference events and identify moments in the play where subtext or symbolism is used to convey key information. For example, on p. 33 Eddie asks Catherine to take off her high-heeled shoes: he does not say why but we see that the shoes symbolise Catherine's growing to be an attractive woman and the subtext is that Eddie does not want Rodolpho seeing this or even feeling that she is wearing the shoes for his benefit.
- **evaluate** means commenting on the quotations you have selected, relating your comments to the question you are tackling. The best candidates are able to see how events through the play develop the themes and ideas that Miller was exploring.

AO2

Explain how **language**, **structure** and **form** contribute to writers' presentation of **ideas**, **themes** and **settings**.

- **language** refers to the lines Miller gives his characters to speak. Look at the first conversation between Eddie and Catherine, when she shows him her new hairstyle and skirt (pp. 13–14). It sounds like a simple everyday conversation, but when Eddie suddenly says 'Now don't aggravate me, Katie' we get a hint of the fact that Eddie does not like to be contradicted by anyone in his own house.
- **structure** refers to the overall shape of the play, as discussed in the *Plot and structure* section of this guide. Remember, for example, that

the passing of hours, days and then weeks are crucial to the way the story unfolds and Eddie changes.

- **form** is more vague when applied to plays generally. In the case of *A View from the Bridge*, the form is heavily influenced by Miller's wish to write a modern version of a classic Greek tragedy. Alfieri's role as narrator and the fact that he is looking back on events from the very start of the play suggests that, just as in those ancient plays, the fate of the protagonist — Eddie — is sealed before the story begins by forces that are too powerful for him to resist. Alfieri speaking directly to the audience is also a version of the narration that features in some Greek tragedies.
- **ideas** refers to the way Miller explores the themes of the play. See the *Themes* section of this guide for detailed discussion of these.

If you were being asked to write about the concepts of justice and the law in the play, you would need to explore:

- The distinction that Alfieri makes from the very start of the play between the legal system of a country and people's ideas of natural justice.
- The fact that law must always be upheld.
- Eddie's inability to understand why the law cannot prevent Rodolpho marrying Catherine. Eddie is asking the lawyer for natural justice, something he cannot give or support.
- Eddie feels a great sense of injustice in the fact that Catherine has fallen in love with an effeminate man: Rodolpho is not a 'real man' like Eddie.
- Alfieri warns Eddie that if he betrays the cousins he will be breaching the code of his people, even though in the eyes of the law Eddie would be doing the right thing.
- At the end of the play Marco demands justice from Eddie; he wants revenge for being betrayed. At the same time Eddie demands what he sees as justice from Marco, he wants Marco to retract the accusation that Eddie informed on the cousins.

By developing these points in detail you are showing the evaluative, insightful and exploratory skills required for an A* grade.

Settings refers to the locations in which the events of the play take place. These are very simple: Alfieri's office, the Carbone apartment and the street outside.

What you will not get marks for

The Assessment Objectives tell you what you *will* get marks for. It is also important to know what you *will not* get marks for:

- **Retelling the story.** You can be sure that the examiner marking your essay knows the play inside out. He or she is probably a teacher

who has taught the play, and will not want to be told the story again. The examiner follows a mark scheme and will probably be referring to 'grade descriptors' giving pointers to the features to be expected from essays at each of the grades. A key feature of the lowest grades is 'retelling the story'. Don't do it!

- **Quoting long passages.** You will waste time and gain no marks by quoting long passages from the play. It will probably not be necessary to quote more than three or four lines at a time.
- **Identifying figures of speech or other features (without further analysis).** You will never gain marks simply for identifying figures of speech, such as the slang or syntax that many of the characters, especially Eddie, use. Similarly, you will gain no marks for just pointing out that Eddie uses a lot of rhetorical questions in his conversation. You will only gain marks by identifying these features and saying why Miller has used them, what they add to our picture of the characters and their world and how effective you think the style of the play is.
- **Giving unsubstantiated opinions**. The examiner will be keen to give you marks for your opinions and reactions to the play, but only if they are supported by reasoned argument and references to the text. Even if you are giving an opinion that is recognised as a correct analysis of the text, it will still be considered unsubstantiated by the examiner if you do not provide evidence to support it.

Hence you will get no marks for writing: 'Marco should be more respectful of Eddie and not make him look foolish by beating him in the chair-lifting contest at the end of Act 1.' You don't give a reason for your opinion.

All the characters in this and every other play are constructs of the playwright's imagination, but a good character is completely believable as a 'real' person. You will get marks for showing how Miller has created characters that have convincing motives for what they do.

Review your learning

1. What is AO1 assessing?
2. What is AO2 assessing?
3. Which board are you doing and what AOs should you be focusing on?
4. What should you not do in your answers?

(See answers on p. 88.)

More interactive questions and answers online.

Sample essays

Six extracts from answers to sample essay questions are provided in this chapter. There are C-grade and A*-grade answers to two different types of questions: a character-based question and a theme-based one. There are also two extracts showing a C- and an A*-grade approach to using quotations. It would be a good idea to read the C-grade essay extracts first and see how you could improve on them. Then read the A*-grade essay extracts. Read the comments on each extract and make sure you understand why some extracts gain a higher grade.

Often the difference between C and A* grades is not content — what you are saying about the play — but the way you use the content to make points and show original thinking. A C-grade answer often contains all the information the examiner is expecting you to know, but it is laid out in a very simple way with quotations used to make quite obvious points, with a lot of retelling of the story and with no clear statement at the start of how the essay will make key points that develop an argument.

Let's look at the beginnings from two essays. The questions ask you to deal with similar key information but are designed for different tiers. Both essays involve writing about Alfieri, but the first is a character-based topic while the second asks you to explore the themes Alfieri helps to develop through the play.

Question 1 (foundation tier)

Write about the role of Alfieri in the play. You should explain:

- how Alfieri acts as a narrator
- how he works as a character within scenes with Eddie and with other characters

C-grade essay

Alfieri is a lawyer who works in Red Hook. He introduces us to the world of the play and the characters we are going to meet. From the way he talks we learn that the story has happened and Eddie is already dead when Alfieri is speaking to us. Alfieri is a narrator as well as a character in the story. He tells us what is happening to other people. He says from the beginning that Eddie's story is just a modern version of a timeless tragedy. **1**

1 This opening paragraph contains core information but in a very simple and rather random way. It would benefit from a clearer explanation of the two roles of Alfieri and the purpose of a narrator. The final point could be developed by adding how Alfieri feels about the timeless story that is going to be played out by Eddie. A brief account of how the essay is planned to answer the question would also help the marker.

We don't learn much about Alfieri himself except that he lived in Italy until he was twenty-five. But he does introduce one of the play's key themes: law versus a code of natural justice. He describes how the community in Red Hook used to settle disputes by violence. Most men in this community regard their honour as very important and if they feel dishonoured they will react violently. Things are becoming more peaceful as people become less Italian and more like Americans. He says 'Now we settle for half, and I like it better. I no longer keep a pistol in my filing cabinet'. **2**

2 The quotation illustrates the point well, but there are more important points about the theme of honour to make first. Explaining why Miller does not think it necessary for us to learn more about Alfieri as a man would add focus to this paragraph.

Now let's look at a higher-tier question that is asking for roughly the same key information, and see how the beginning of an essay can work to gain the higher grade.

Question 2 (higher tier)

Explore the two roles that Alfieri plays in *A View from the Bridge*.

A*-grade essay

Miller begins the play with a long speech from Alfieri, a lawyer who works within the Red Hook community. He shares the same background as the other characters in the drama but appears — until the last moments of the play — to have left behind much of the southern Italian culture with its focus on honour and justice that drives Eddie and Marco. Indeed he suggests that many other people in the community feel like he does: 'Now we settle for half and I like it better.' (p. 12) The use of 'we' suggests a shared change of attitude.

Alfieri only engages with other characters three times: his two interviews with Eddie and his legal intervention to allow Marco and Rodolpho to be freed to work before their deportation hearing. Yet these three appearances, the advice he gives Eddie and his releasing the cousins, have profound effects on the unfolding tragedy. His personal journey is that by the end of the play he questions whether he has completely left behind the kind of beliefs that have caused the play's tragic ending.

Alfieri fulfils another key function and role: he is a narrator who speaks directly to the audience at key moments through the play...

Although this opening does not explain how the student is planning to construct the full essay, it reveals a good overall grasp of the play, of Alfieri's role within the story and his own character. Reference to his three appearances shows a clear grasp of the story structure of the play, and the final comment about Alfieri's view of himself shows understanding of the need for all characters to be changed by the events of the play. The first paragraph is full of information that shows the student can take an overview of the whole play and not become stuck on details or on just retelling the story. The final sentence from the extract is the opening line of a second introductory paragraph which would go on to sum up Alfieri's role as a narrator.

Now let's look at two more questions. Again they ask for similar key information to be presented, but this time they are asking, at least in part, for the student to focus on themes in the play rather than on characters.

Question 3 (foundation tier)

Show how different characters are driven by the ideas of justice and honour to do things in the story.
Write about Eddie, Marco and Alfieri.

C-grade essay

Eddie is the main character in the play. He has a strong sense of duty and of doing the right thing to look after his family. When he is challenged about this he becomes dangerous. Marco too is driven by a desire to do things to look after his family back in Italy. Both these characters have a similar idea of what it is to be a man. Alfieri is a lawyer and so he ought to have a different idea of justice, yet by the end of the play he is wondering if he is really more like Eddie than he wants to admit.

This opening paragraph contains some important information about each of the characters that the question asks the student to write about. It would have been better to have introduced the theme of natural law versus justice before giving a little sketch of each character. Nothing that is said about the characters is backed up with any reference to evidence. The student's approach to the question is typical of a C-grade answer: key information and ideas are identified but expressed very simply and without the potential for development into more original and thoughtful commentary. .

Question 4 (higher tier)

Show how Miller explores the theme of justice in the play through the actions of key characters.

Some years before he was a successful playwright and wrote *A View from the Bridge*, Miller worked in the New York docks with men who, like Eddie and Marco, were Italian immigrants. He was keen to write a play that both told a powerful personal tragic story and explored ideas that he saw were important in the lives of these men. One of the key themes in this play is the difference between upholding the law and following a personal need for natural justice. It is their desire for honour and justice that drives Eddie and Marco to the play's fatal climax. It is Alfieri's ability to understand both this kind of justice and the need to obey laws in order to live a safer and less volatile life that allows the play to explore this complex theme.

The opening sentence shows knowledge of the context of the play. Instead of going straight into accounts of how certain characters are driven by ideas of natural justice or a need to respect the law, this opening paragraph focuses on the quite complex nature

of the ideas that Miller wants to make us think about. It demonstrates that the student has a clear understanding of these. The three characters who are most tied to the theme of natural justice in the play are introduced. This opening suggests the student is confident about their grasp of the key information the play contains which they need to construct a thorough answer to the question..

The final two sample sections of essays show you how a C-grade answer uses quotations, and compares this to the use of quotations to make key points in an A* essay. Both these sample sections would come in the middle of an essay, where the student was using quotations to develop arguments and evidence their ideas.

Question 5 (foundation tier)

How does Miller create different voices for his characters?
Write about Eddie, Alfieri and Rodolpho.

C-grade essay

This extract would come in that part of the essay where a distinction between the way Alfieri and Eddie speak is being explored, by looking at their exchanges in their two meetings in Alfieri's office.

We don't see Alfieri engaging with any other character until Eddie comes to visit him to ask for advice in Act 1. Several weeks have passed since the cousins arrived and Eddie is getting angry about Rodolpho's interest in Catherine. Eddie wants to know if there is a law he can use to stop Rodolpho marrying his niece.

Alfieri's way of speaking now is less poetic but still clearly different from Eddie's. Alfieri speaks calmly and logically. He speaks far less than Eddie, usually just one line at a time, which is surprising given that Eddie has come to ask for advice. 'Eddie, I'm a lawyer. I can only deal in what's provable.' This shows his lawyer's training. Eddie does not like what Alfieri tells him and becomes angry, but Alfieri remains calm. When Alfieri comes close to suggesting he knows that Eddie is attracted to Catherine, Eddie becomes furious: 'What're you talkin' about, marry me! I don't know what the hell you're talkin' about!' Alfieri never tells Eddie that perhaps he wants more than he as a lawyer can give him.

There is a lot that can be said about the first meeting between Eddie and Alfieri (pp. 45–49). Some important points about the difference between the two men are touched on here, but they are not developed. The quotations are not well chosen and are not explained. Seeing the balance of lines between Eddie and Alfieri shows some analysis of the way the scene is constructed but in fact each character has one or more quite long speeches and it is around these that the scene unfolds. Little mention is made in this extract of how what the characters say to each other develops our understanding of their characters, motives and thinking.

Now let's look at an extract from a higher-tier question that also asks students to write about the differences between the way characters talk, and where the same meeting between Eddie and Alfieri is used as a source for quotations to develop ideas.

Question 6 (higher tier)

A View from the Bridge is written in a naturalistic style, yet Miller creates distinct voices for his main characters. Identify key places in the play where this contrast of voices is used to dramatic effect.

A*-grade essay

This extract deals with the same scene of the play as the previous question, but shows greater analysis and a much better use of quotations to develop points.

Miller uses the differences between the voices of Eddie and Alfieri to add to the drama of their first meeting at the lawyer's office in Act 1. There is a clear structure to this scene that shows Eddie's growing frustration when he learns there is no law to stop Rodolpho marrying Catherine, and Alfieri's increasing alarm as he realises just how desperate Eddie is and why.

For the first two pages of the scene the men speak for no more than two lines at a time. The effect is of short sharp exchanges:

'EDDIE: The guy ain't right, Mr Alfieri.

ALFIERI: What do you mean?

EDDIE: I mean he ain't right.

ALFIERI: I don't get you.'

Miller is showing Eddie as a man who is struggling to say what he feels, to express things about himself in a way that he is not used to or comfortable with. He is showing Alfieri as a man who is struggling to recognise just what advice he is being asked to provide.

As the scene develops Eddie become more desperate to express himself, and then Alfieri, realising Eddie's passion, becomes very keen to show him that he has to let Catherine go for everyone's well-being. As the drama increases, so both men have longer and more passionate speeches. Alfieri tries hard to convince Eddie he has to let Catherine go without saying what he thinks will happen if he doesn't. 'The child has to grow up and go away, and the man has to learn to forget. Because after

all, Eddie — what other way can it end?' Alfieri shows his legal training here in his careful use of words. He talks about the situation in general terms, 'the child...the man', so creating a distance between what he is saying and the Carbone household; and he asks Eddie a rhetorical question, a device that invites him to think about the truth of what he is being told rather than provide an answer. This contrasts with the following speech, a long one from Eddie which is full of passion and anger and name-calling: he calls Rodolpho 'a son-of-a-bitch punk' who 'puts his dirty filthy hands on her like a goddam thief'. The contrast between Alfieri's warning and advice and Eddie's anger creates much of the drama of the scene.

This extract shows good understanding of how a playwright creates drama not just through the content of what characters say to one another but also through the way they say it. Quotations are well used to support points of analysis. There is much more that could be said about the subtext and the content of the two big speeches that are referred to, but this extract focuses accurately on how the characters are written to sound distinct from one another.

Context (p. 12)

1 The context of a play is the cultural, social and political world in which it was written and against the background of which it should be studied. In the case of *A View from the Bridge* this is the Italian immigrant community in New York in (probably) the late 1930s.
2 Italian immigrants had been coming to America since the 19th century and stories of a better life had been filtering back to Italy for generations. Many Italians living in poverty had relations who were already in America. Hollywood films were popular all over Europe and promoted the idea of American cities as exciting and glamorous places.
3 Illegal immigrants could not get employment where they had to produce tax details and identity papers, so they were at the mercy of unscrupulous employers who hired them illegally and often subjected them to very poor pay and conditions.
4 'Ordinary Americans' were divided (as are people are today who are citizens of various countries which immigrants are entering) into those who were happy to see people come to boost the labour market and enrich the culture, and those who felt that immigrants, especially illegal ones, were a danger and a burden.

Plot and structure (p. 29)

1 On the day the play starts Catherine gets the offer of a job and the cousins arrive. These are both significant events in the Carbone household and a good place for Miller to start the action of the play.
2 It tells the audience in graphic detail the powerful code of honour that the community live by and which the Carbones appear to approve of.
3 Eddie dislikes Rodolpho's blond hair, his easy way around women, his singing, cooking and sewing skills and his ability to make people laugh: all of which could be summed up as effeminate qualities in Eddie's eyes. Most of all, and probably triggering all of these things, Eddie primarily dislikes the fact that Catherine and Rodolpho appear almost instantly attracted to each other. Rodolpho is young, full of fun and not weighed down by the sense of duty and hard work that men like Eddie and Marco live by. In addition, Catherine does not seem to have had much experience of men and potential boyfriends, especially ones who come into the house, sing and help her make clothes!

4 Miller wants to show that Eddie is a good if very simple man who is genuinely hurt by things that are happening in his family, even if he cannot acknowledge his own darker motives for this sense of rejection. Placing him in a good light just before he does the worst thing a man in his position, in his community, can do, adds to the drama of Eddie's fall into anger and betrayal.
5 Marco is a man of few words and we have already had, at the end of Act 1, a long scene with much talking between the characters in the house. Marco's dramatic gesture of physical strength is a warning to Eddie that, if Eddie attacks Rodolpho again, he will have to deal with Marco. Eddie is defeated, literally overshadowed, by Marco in his own house.
6 Catherine has sided with Rodolpho, transferring her affection from Eddie to the man she wants to marry. Eddie has become isolated. He cannot share his thoughts with anyone. It is significant that he is drunk at the start of Act 2; up to now we have imagined him too serious, too focused on work and family, to do such a frivolous thing.
7 Alfieri had to weigh up the risk that Marco might seek revenge against the opportunity that he could create for him to work until his deportation. Alfieri did not know Marco at all, and perhaps does not realise how strong Marco's belief in natural justice and how self-destructive his sense of honour are.

Characterisation (p. 46)

1 At the start of the play Catherine has a very childlike but genuine affection for her uncle, which he does nothing to discourage. She may be beginning to see — and enjoy — the effect she is having on him as an attractive young woman, maybe without even fully realising that this is sexually provocative. By the end of the play she has turned completely against him with the same force with which she so recently loved him.
2 Eddie regards Alfieri as more than a lawyer. Eddie feels he is an educated and experienced man who can offer advice. However, Eddie becomes angry when Alfieri does not tell him what he wants to hear. Alfieri is the first person in the play to block Eddie's wishes. Alfieri does not really know Eddie well, but he admires the kind of man he is, and he admires something about Eddie's individual drive and passion, even when that leads to his death.
3 Beatrice sees what effect Catherine's growing into womanhood is having on Eddie and wants her out of the house to prevent Eddie being tempted to act on his still secret desires. Beatrice also suspects that if

Catherine is out of Eddie's sight, then he might become interested in her sexually again.

4 Rodolpho is part of Eddie's extended family and it shames Eddie if people make fun of him, even if he himself does not like Rodolpho and mocks him for the same reasons as his workmates.
5 To set up as many differences as possible between the characters of Rodolpho and Eddie.
6 To test Rodolpho, to find out if he loves her for herself or if he only wants to marry in order to get citizenship to stay legally in America.
7 Eddie has to keep up the pretence that he has been wrongly accused of betrayal, even though everyone knows he has done this. His sense of honour will not allow him to try to make peace with Marco or even apologise. He may also be so deluded, so in the grip of anger at what is happening with Catherine and Rodolpho, that he really believes he is the injured party.

Themes (p. 52)

1 The theme of natural justice versus law is the most important theme of the play. It drives the main character to his tragic end. It is the only theme directly referred to in Alfieri's introductory speech as narrator.
2 The theme of love is timeless. Ideas explored in the theme of natural justice and the law regarding what an immigrant brings from their country to a new home is also relevant to many times and places.
3 Miller had worked with men like Eddie Carbone. As a writer, he was interested in making modern versions of timeless stories.
4 Miller had personal knowledge of the Italian community in Red Hook and knew it was one where ideas of honour and justice were very strongly held.
5 Alfieri presents this theme directly to the audience through his role as a narrator in his speeches at the start and end of the play. Alfieri also links the impending tragedy that is driven by this theme to Eddie in his two shorter addresses to the audience in Act 1 (pp. 26, 33–34).

Style (p. 60)

1 Rodolpho enjoys telling stories, usually with some humour in them. His English is not perfect but he tries hard to be expressive and descriptive. His conversation is much freer and less guarded than Eddie's or Marco's, and his enthusiasm makes him sound like the younger man that he is.
2 Alfieri's speeches as narrator to the audience are more thoughtful and poetic than the exchanges between the other characters. They give a sense of gravity to the play.

3 Eddie is not an educated man. He also works hard to conceal his true feelings and motives for much of the play. His desperation to find words to express himself bursts to the surface with great force through his first meeting with Alfieri. 'Please, Mr Alfieri. I'm tryin' to bring out my thoughts here.' (p. 47)
4 Miller writes lines for most characters using apostrophes and respellings to indicate how their pronunciations differ from standard English; an example of the latter is 'summat' for 'something'.

Tackling the assessments (p. 73)

1 Use quotations to evidence your argument and opinions.
2 Identify the point that you want to make (within your overall essay plan). Look for evidence and a quotation to support it from the relevant part of the play. Explain how the evidence supports your point.
3 Foundation-tier questions usually have a number of bullet point hints to help you plan your answer. Use them as the basis of your essay plan.
4 Underline key words in the question.
5 What is the writer aiming to do? How do they go about doing it? Have they been successful?

Assessment Objectives and skills (p. 78)

1 AO1 is assessing how well you can 'Respond to texts critically and imaginatively; select and evaluate relevant textual detail to illustrate and support interpretations'.
2 AO2 is assessing how well you can 'Explain how language, structure and form contribute to writers' presentation of ideas, themes and settings'.
3 Answer this question by identifying the AOs your examining board is asking you to work with.
4 You should you not retell the story in your own words, quote long passages without very good reasons and explanations, identify figures of speech or other stylistic features without further analysis, or give unsubstantiated opinions about the play.

Notes